Flight of the Pangolin

Flight of the Pangolin

The Pangolin Republic: Book 1

Michael Moutinho

Aberdyne Books

http://www.thepangolinrepublic.com

Cover art by Vitaliy Ostashchenko

First Printing, 2024

For Danielle, who read my outline for a sci-fi webseries
and said, "Why don't you write this as a book?"

SFS PANGOLIN • 5th COALITION BATTLE FLEET • 1200 MK FROM PRAHARI

Commander Chapman stepped onto the command deck and into an uproar of comm noise. Most notably above the din, Coalition Central Command was receiving a status report from their diplomatic ship, the SFS *Calumet*.

"Negative, Command One. All frequencies, no response."

The 5th Fleet had set up a defensive formation blocking the Sanzoku's approach trajectory, with the SFS *Calumet* as the tip of the spear. It was hoped that here, at the heart of human civilization, at the doorstep of the old, dead homeworld Yaodong, the silent attackers who had laid waste to so many colony worlds would finally be willing to talk. To bargain. At the very least, to listen to the feeble pleas of an outmatched foe.

For now, the ships of both fleets hung staring at each other in the shadow of the Moon, Prahari, each separated by nothing but an imaginary line and joined by a (hopefully) mutual reluctance to provoke the other.

The Sanzoku had brought their brand of wholesale death to the solar system just over a year ago, but this was the first time any human had encountered their ships without being immediately vaporized, which was, in itself, a hopeful sign. The list of colonies and outposts completely wiped off the map was extensive; the list of casualties was heavy with family of officers and recent enlistees in this hastily cobbled together Coalition military. For so many in the fleet, this had become personal.

"I can't believe we're still just sitting here," muttered Lieutenant Drake. It had been over ten hours since the fleet had taken position; six since the Sanzoku ships arrived. Now even Drake, the unflappable tactical officer, was getting antsy. Under the circumstances, some level of fatigue was inevitable. Or maybe Drake could taste the opportunity for revenge. Did he have family lost in the Sanzoku attacks? Chapman didn't know.

"Stow that noise, Lieutenant!" he replied. As first officer, Chapman took his job of maintaining crew morale seriously. Revenge was a pointless idea anyway, he'd decided after many, many nights of soul-searching.

Captain Houlihan gave Drake a dismissive "Stand down, Drake," and continued watching the imaging table at the center of the command deck, which showed a realtime tactical holographic display of what looked like a formation of flying insects. This hive of activity represented the Coalition fleet, with its capital ships standing stoically in place surrounded by wings of patrolling fighters.

Houlihan was particularly interested in the fleet's left flank. To Chapman's eye, the LSS *Lesotho* and the PSS *Odesa* were just slightly out of position.

The comm let out a three-note tone, signaling a transmission from Central Command. "Command One to fleet," announced the designated voice of Central Command (if Chapman were to guess, he'd say it was Admiral Fennell), "Let's give them one last chance. I don't want history saying we didn't try every avenue. All ships, attempt one more comm try; use all conceivable frequencies. Morse code, semaphore, sign language if you have to. Command One out."

Chapman's orders were clear. "Lieutenant Coleman, you heard the order. All frequencies."

The captain looked up from the imaging table. "Commander Chapman, why don't you do the honors?"

"Me, sir?"

The captain raised an arm up theatrically. "If you would be so kind."

Chapman had so much to learn from Captain Houlihan about leadership. In a pressure situation, with the crew on edge but fading after six hours of battle readiness, why not change things up in a way that doesn't affect protocol at all? Chapman proceeded to the comm station, where Lt. Coleman offered him the hand mike. "Unidentified ships, this is Commander Maxwell Chapman of the Satellite Federation ship *Pangolin* requesting communication with anyone able to negotiate a peaceful settlement. Further...incursions will not be tolerated, but we seek a peaceful resolution to the current conflict. Please respond." He repeated the message in other base languages - Sperant, Dominionese, a few others - and had Coleman broadcast in a few numeric and base codes, because those were far outside his skill set.

"Why are they not attacking?" Drake suddenly blurted out. Drake's outburst worried Chapman; the tactical officer was typically the one crew member they could always count on to be rock solid. Nerves were frayed all over the ship, understandable on an operation like this: a patchwork fleet embarking on a last-ditch suicide mission to save the human race from extinction. But in the past, Drake had always been the most professional of the officers on this ragtag crew.

"Steady, Drake," replied Captain Houlihan in a calm, measured voice. "Who knows how long it will take them to process our message? I hate to say it, but we could be here for a long while. Coleman, is imaging up yet?"

Lieutenant Coleman checked her display readouts. "Intel satellites are fixing orbit now, sir, and fighter imaging is complete. We're at 87 percent resolution so far, Cap."

"That's good enough," said Houlihan. "Let's see it."

The imager widened out in scope, shrinking the fleet and slowly resolving a new, much larger image across from it. Three Sanzoku ships - each one a good twice the size of Hong Dominion's *Chrysanthemum*, the largest ship left in the Coalition fleet - hovered over the tac display table, dwarfing the fleet.

Houlihan whistled in awe.

Pires, up in the cockpit, let out a quiet "filho de fleuma" as his own imager resolved the enemy ships, and Drake seethed quietly at his station.

Chapman stared at the image of the ships as they slowly clarified. He thought of Lex for the first time in nearly five minutes. Was this the last thing she saw, before the end? One of these massive metallic spheres bearing down on Outpost Orange? Better to stow such thoughts, for now.

The Command tone broadcast over the comm. "Command One to all ships..." the voice paused, a different voice from the last. There may have been a resigned sigh in there, as well. "Discontinue current hails. Launch fighter group Alpha, Kingfisher Five formation. Broadcast orders to unidentified craft: Thirty seconds to begin retreat or they will be fired upon. This will be our last attempt at communication. Command One out."

Houlihan straightened his posture. "Chapman, do it. Pires, back us off. Fleet coverage formation Kingfisher Five."

"Kingfisher Five, aye sir," Pires parroted.

Chapman, with a mild reluctance not missed by the captain, raised the hand mike to his face once again. Chapman knew how to obey orders, even when he didn't agree with them. Far be it for him to question the orders of Central Command, but they'd probably just sealed humankind's death warrant. Thirty seconds?

"Unidentified ships, this is Commander Chapman of the Satellite Federation ship *Pangolin* requesting your immediate withdrawal from this star system. You have thirty seconds to begin compliance measures. Failure to do so will be met with force."

Pires flew the ship into the new formation as the fleet closed in on the Sanzoku ships. The command deck was silent.

Fighter Group Alpha's CAG broke in on the comm. "Alpha One to Command One. Fighters are go, awaiting orders."

"Acknowledged, Alpha One. Stand by." There were multiple voices arguing indistinctly in the background of Central Command's transmission. A fine time for the Coalition to unravel...

"That's not a good sign," muttered Coleman under her breath. Chapman silently agreed.

To Coleman's horror, Houlihan heard her. "Everything's on the line, Lieutenant. Tensions are high. They may never be higher in our lifetimes." He addressed the entire command deck. "But we've got a job to do. I intend to be the first captain to survive a Sanzoku attack. And I intend to bring all of you with me." Standard Houlihan; he had a great future in the theater once this battle was over.

A new voice broke in on the comm to Alpha One. "Command Actual to Alpha One. Fire in five seconds on my mark. Mark."

"They're gonna do it," Drake said. "They're really gonna do it."

The Coalition was desperate for any edge against the Sanzoku once word came that their ships were heading for Prahari. In that spirit, the fleet was equipped with experimental weapons: missiles with quantum shielding that could, supposedly, penetrate any solid matter. These missiles were still very early in the test stage, but due to the gravity of the situation they were approved for use in this action. The *Pangolin* had about a hundred of them in her hold, and Alpha Group was armed with ten per fighter.

Whether Drake was referring to the potential destruction of the Sanzoku ships, or to the use of these experimental missiles, was anyone's guess.

"Imaging," Houlihan called out. "Detail on Alpha Group."

The fighter group had reached the designated launch point and fired. The missiles, dozens of small, red cylinders of light on the imager, sped toward their targets...and described beautiful upward arcs as they reversed back on to the fighter group.

"Command Actual to Alpha One, status." There was a distinct edge in her voice.

The edge in Central Command's voice was nothing compared to the pants-loading fear in Alpha One's. "Target lock system was engaged - is still engaged - on enemy ships. Missiles appear to be ignoring lock and are self-acquiring targets within Alpha Group, repeat, within Alpha Group. Taking evasive maneuvers." The fighters danced on the imager, chased by the tiny red cylinders of death that they themselves had launched. And as they danced, the fighters' evasive maneuvers began bringing them closer to the Coalition fleet.

"Pires," Houlihan shouted, "back off from formation, route two five."

"Two five, aye sir."

"Alpha One, this is Command Actual, break off-"

"Command, advise the fleet - evasive maneuvers, missiles inbound-" and then Alpha One was reduced to static.

"Tactical, keep an eye on those missiles," shouted Houlihan.

On the imager, a few dozen missiles caught up with the fighters they'd been chasing, the craft blinking out of existence. "There goes half of Alpha Group," Chapman said.

"And the *Caithness*!" exclaimed Drake.

In the melee, the SFS *Caithness*, one of the Satellite Federation's capital ships, had tried to close the gap between the fleet and the Sanzoku ships, drawing fire from some of the errant quantum missiles away from the fighters. A few hits to the drive section had left the *Caithness* listing and almost entirely out of control.

"It was too close to the line," Chapman observed, "why didn't it back off when the fighters engaged?"

"Schultz always was overconfident. She was trying to make the 'Ness a target for the missiles so the fighters could re-engage." He paused. "Coleman," he shouted, "tell the fleet to back off to-" he indicated a point on the image, and the imager pulled up the coordinates, "347.4 by 85, zero Z."

"You don't think-" started Chapman.

"Schultz is going out in a blaze of glory," Houlihan confirmed.

"Well," replied Chapman, "if this is humanity's last stand, at least we'll take a few of them with us."

The crew watched as the *Caithness* listed directly into one of the Sanzoku ships, drive section first. The explosion obliterated both ships, and the ensuing shockwave sent the fleet, including the *Pangolin*, reeling. "Damage report!" Chapman shouted, once the ship had stopped spinning.

Drake had fully composed himself and was now filled with the steely resolve he was known for. "Imaging and comm systems are down." He checked his readouts. "Sir, we have incoming."

"Quantum missiles?"

"No, Commander," Drake replied, "the remaining fighters are flying directly into the fleet, at speed!"

Houlihan was calmly brushing himself off. "Pires, evasive action. Drake, give Pires as much space as you can, and plot a ramming solution."

"Sir?" Drake asked.

Houlihan smiled at Chapman, and clarified to Drake, "Keep it in your back pocket for now, Lieutenant." To Chapman, "At least we know they're not completely invincible."

Coleman exclaimed, "Comm system is back up!"

The comm exploded with a transmission from Central Command at a high volume: "Command One to all ships: break off attack. Repeat, break off and regroup at-" The transmission was abruptly cut off and replaced with audio static.

"Signals are being jammed on all frequencies," Coleman reported.

Houlihan was none too pleased. "Status of enemy ships?"

"One craft destroyed," replied Drake. "Two remaining, holding their position." He got a new report from his readouts. "Sir, our starboard guns are down."

"Fire in Ordnance Bay Two," Chapman reported. "Damage Control is responding."

"Condition of the fleet?" Houlihan demanded.

Drake shook his head. "We have incomplete imaging data, but from what I can tell the fleet is in total chaos."

"Pires, report."

"I'm a little busy right now, Cap! No, no, no, no..."

"Sir, should we fire our quantum missiles?" Drake asked.

"After what just happened?" Chapman countered.

The crew was thrown around the command deck by an especially large hit.

"Report!" Chapman shouted as he slowly got to his feet.

"Sir," reported Drake, "that starboard collision was the PSS *Ghent.*"

"Pires?"

"Sorry!" called out Pires from the cockpit.

"So much for the League's Coalition of Worlds," said Houlihan, ruefully.

"Sir, are you ok?" asked Chapman.

"Yeah, Chaps, I think so. Why?"

Coleman saw it too. It was hard not to, really, even with his dark skin and the dimness of the command deck's tactical lighting. "Your nose is bleeding, Cap."

It was a gusher, running down from his left nostril and dripping to the floor from his top lip, but Captain Houlihan didn't seem to notice anything wrong.

Coleman stood up from her station to get the captain a medpack, but had to grab the nearest crash-handle to keep from falling. "I'm so dizzy all of a sudden..."

Drake put his hands to his temples. "Ugh, my head!"

Another large explosion rocked the ship. A section of ceiling-mounted coolant conduit piping came loose and fell directly on Chapman's head, dazing him. He stumbled and fell to the deck.

"Chapman!" Houlihan exclaimed. He gingerly made his way to the comm station, where Coleman was now writhing on the deck in pain. "Damage Control and med team to the command deck. Half the ceiling just caved in on Chapman...coolant leak...looks like he hit his head pretty hard..." Houlihan fell to the floor, not far from Coleman.

As she was joined by her captain, with her eyes, ears and nose bleeding profusely, Coleman could only think to ask, "What is this?"

As Chapman lost consciousness, he could hear Drake reply with an unintelligible scream.

2

FORT NANDI • COLLINSTOWN • PRAHARI • PRAHARI REPUBLIC

Chapman awoke to the sound of electronic beeps and whines. The smell that hit his nose was overbearingly clean, with an underlying hint of urine. He did not need to open his eyes to know that he was in a hospital.

Maybe if he kept his eyes shut, he could somehow deny this reality.

He heard someone enter the room; he figured it was finally time to open his eyes. The room was small, and he was facing a window with a decent view of Collinstown, easily identifiable by the Late American utilitarian architecture. He could see the iconic dome of the City Commons complex, as well as several of Prahari's famed white helical spires. His was the only bed in the room, and there was a small washroom off to one side. Off in the doorway stood a nurse, watching Chapman intently. He poked his head back out the door, yelling down the hallway.

"He's waking up. Get the Admiral." The nurse ran up to Chapman's bedside. "Captain Chapman, how are you feeling, sir?"

"Like I've been asleep for ages." He tried to move, but found himself attached by tubes and wires to the sources of the beeps and whines around him, which were of course protesting via more of those same sounds. "What? What?" he asked the machines, irritatedly. His brain was not yet firing on all thrusters.

The nurse tended to the machines, silencing some of the louder alerts. "Try not to move too much yet. Your skull is still healing, so you may experience some headaches and dizziness." He lifted the bedsheet and unplugged a feeding tube that was jacked into a new plughole in Chapman's abdomen. Chapman stared at his torso in horror. "That's...not permanent," the nurse said.

"What happened?" Chapman asked, leaning his head back on the pillow and closing his eyes.

"Well, sir, because of the length of your incapacity-"

"Not the food plug, I get that. Everything else. How long was I out? What's the status of my ship? How's the war going?" Maybe if I keep my eyes closed, he thought, I could go back to sleep. Maybe for good, this time. Maybe this is some kind of fever dream and all I need to do is truly wake up.

"Best to let the Admiral tell you," the nurse replied. "She should be here in a moment."

As if on cue, Admiral Vanakar walked into the room. Even if she hadn't been dressed in a red Satellite Federation blazer adorned with every possible medal given out by Federation Fleet Command and the Coalition's Central Command, by her bearing alone one would be able to surmise that Jemma Vanakar was a five-star admiral and highest-ranking officer in the Federation fleet. Another sign - the half-dozen or so people following her at a few paces: recorders, personal comm officers, a chronicler, even a medic, as the admiral was pushing sixty. But it was her bearing that alerted Chapman, even in his hazy state, to salute involuntarily.

"Don't get up, Captain," she said to Chapman. She then turned to the nurse. "Give us a few minutes. All of you," the last bit addressing her train of followers. The nurse left last, closing the door behind him. "Captain Chapman, I'll answer your questions, but you'll have to answer some of mine. I realize you just woke up, but this is vitally important."

"Commander, ma'am."

"What?"

"I'm not a captain, ma'am."

"Are you turning down a promotion, Mister Chapman?"

This was all a bit much for him. Even in his hazy state, he immediately realized he could retire comfortably on a captain's pension, with disability pay. "No, ma'am, I am not."

"Good. A lot has happened since the Battle of the Prahari Line - that's what they're calling it now - one of them is, you made Captain. Congratulations. You weren't awake for the ceremony but we imaged it for you; talk to my chronicler later." She paused. "I'm sure you'd like to know what happened in the battle. Where is your ship, your crew. How everything turned out."

"We won?" Chapman guessed, since he was still alive.

Vanakar paused. "We didn't lose," she replied, diplomatically. "Of the three enemy ships we met at the Prahari Line, one was destroyed. The other two...left." She sat in a chair next to his bed.

"And the fleet?"

She sighed. "What really happened out there, Chapman? From what we've been able to piece together, the fighters' missile locks were somehow overridden remotely, but we didn't detect any jamming or transmission that would have affected the targeting systems. Then the pilots lost all control, and the fighters themselves started attacking the fleet."

Chapman thought hard. The memories were slowly returning. "We tried to fire on the fighters as they came at us, since the pilots said they no longer had contact with their ships. Some of them were crashing right into the capital ships. The Caithness had been hit in the drive section and-"

"The Caithness took out one of the enemy ships. By some miracle, it was enough. The two remaining ships left without turning Prahari into a lifeless rock like all the others. There have been no more like Outpost Orange, or New Gilder or Kamakura or Herschel. We haven't been attacked since.

"That's the good news."

Chapman braced himself. "And the bad news?"

"Casualties were...high. The Caithness took out the enemy ship, but the resulting shockwave destroyed or crippled most of the Coalition fleet. Rogue missiles and fighters made short work of most of the crippled ships. And then there was the *Pangolin*. Did you know that your ship was the only one to survive the battle even remotely intact? No," she stopped him when it looked like Chapman was trying to answer, "of course you didn't, you were out, it's a rhetorical question."

Admiral Vanakar looked down at her hands. She'd been in the service for over forty years, and this part never got any easier. "Captain, we lost a lot of ships. Not just the Federation, but the whole Coalition. Out of that whole fleet, the only ship we managed to salvage was yours. And from that ship... you were the only survivor."

Maxwell Chapman had gone through life with the belief that anything was possible. But the idea that an entire fleet of ships - thousands of officers, crew, pilots, and support staff - all died, but he had lived? Even without a concussion he'd have trouble comprehending all of this. He could only manage a weak, "How?"

The admiral took a deep breath. "The matter is classified. I realize you are owed an explanation; I do. But until we can explain what happened to your fellow crew members...unless you have something to contribute?"

He rubbed the back of his neck, exhaling slowly. "I can't think of anything."

Admiral Vanakar looked him over. Was she looking for clues, or to pin the loss on me? he thought. She stood. "Well, it's early days, you've only been conscious for a few minutes, after all. If you think of something, please let me know. For now, rest up, and if you can pass a medical in a few months, who knows what the future may hold for you. We'll do what we can for your privacy, but try to stay out of the press."

"The press?" Chapman had always considered himself one of the most boring people he'd ever known; the idea that anyone in the press would have an interest in him was completely insane.

Halfway out the door, the Admiral paused, turned to him and replied, "You're the only survivor of the decisive battle of what is now being called the Sanzoku War. You're gonna be in the history books...Captain."

The admiral left Chapman alone with his many thoughts. From his hospital bed, he looked out at the skyline of Collinstown. For the average citizen, life had probably already returned to business as usual.

Another nurse, a pretty young woman, arrived to take his vitals. The machines beeped and warbled as she checked their readouts. Occasionally she pressed a button, flipped a few switches.

She addressed him, breaking his thoughtless reverie. "Captain, can you extend your left arm towards me, please?"

"Sure," he replied, complying with her request. He watched her apply a few new sensor pads to his pulse points. She seemed distant, and he certainly wasn't his usual charming self at the moment, but he needed to understand. "Do you know anything about what happened to my crew?"

She was reluctant to respond. "I wasn't involved in any of that, sir. Besides, everything on that topic is classified."

Chapman sensed a "but" somewhere in there, as if she wanted to talk, but her professionalism (or her orders, or just good sense) was preventing it. He pressed on. "I understand, but I just thought that, you know, since I was there and all..."

"Well, there's nothing official that I know about, just some unconfirmed reports...rumors, that kind of thing. But I don't think-"

"I understand. It's just that...whatever it is, I'd like to know." She seemed conflicted, and turned back to her machines. "Please."

She studied the readout on a pulse monitor intently. "I know a couple of the guys who worked in the basement. You know, the crematorium? They said...they said all the bodies that came back from the battle had the same - I'm sorry. They said it was like their brains were liquefied." She turned to him, her eyes glassy with welling tears. "I don't know if it's true, sir, I can't imagine...I hope it's not true, but that's what they told me."

A new weapon from the Sanzoku? A side effect of the shockwave from their ship's destruction? He nodded to her. "Thank you for telling me, even if it is unsubstantiated."

"No one deserves to die that way..." She shook her head, sniffled loudly. She paused for a brief eternity, her machines long forgotten. "They say you had a friend? That she was lost at Outpost Orange in the first attack. I lost my brother at Manipur."

"I'm sorry."

"Does it get any easier, as time goes by? I'm sorry, I'm getting too personal." She collected a few data cards from the monitor units, more busywork than anything. "I just...I wanted to thank you for your efforts."

"No, it's alright," Chapman replied, catching her lightly by the forearm as she turned to leave. "I spent the better part of the past year thinking about nothing else but hunting down and destroying whatever it was that tore through the system. The Sanzoku. I think that some of my crew may have been after revenge right down to the end, but I wasn't interested in that, not after a while. I don't know...revenge doesn't solve anything, it doesn't bring people back, it doesn't make things right. But if we could stop it from happening again, that would be worthwhile. And I put all my energies toward that, and you know, now that I'm thinking about it, I didn't really give myself time to grieve. I probably just used the whole thing as an excuse to distract myself from my loss, you know? Anyway, I'm sorry we didn't stop them before they got to Manipur, but I honestly don't have any more answers than you do. I hope...I hope it gets easier, for all of us."

The nurse nodded, wiping away a few tears. "Thank you, Captain." She composed herself as best she could. "Everything checks out for now, someone will be in to look in on you in a few hours. Until then, try to get some rest." She left, closing the door behind her.

He looked around the empty hospital room, packed with machines working full tilt to keep him alive. For the first time since before he met Lex at a tea stand next to the sauropod pen at the Hibernia Zoo & Menagerie, he wondered if it was worth the effort.

3

COURTYARD OF THE SUNSET • IMPERIAL PALACE • MOUNT HAIYUAN • HONG PRIME

The Dauphin Kwan Li sat in his customary spot, a bench near the edge of the Pool of the Cranes, and contemplated. From here, he had watched countless sunsets over his 23 standard years in the palace court. The view from here - at the top of the highest point in the solar system - was grandiose, to say the least.

Mount Haiyuan was the center of the Infinite City, a sprawl starting along its impossibly long low-angle incline, radiating out across the entirety of Hong Prime. Once a red planet, its surface was now almost completely covered in storey after storey of the same stylish metal and glass skyscrapers that populated the dozens of other worlds of the solar system. The sides of its canyons were the pale steel faces of underground industrial facilities. In a nod to the past, the Shadeshield maintained the world's historic red tint from space.

Civilization in the solar system owed itself almost entirely to Shadeshield technology. For the first hundred years or so following the diaspora, when the old euroligarchs and Chinese split up the inner system between them and led the exodus from Yaodong (what became euphemistically known in the annals of history as the Noble Egress), people lived in Hong Prime's sealed dome cities, or in Cerigo's underground caves. Gravity was native and nonstandard. The development of the ionic pressfield made control of gravity possible on a planetary scale, and a variety of important tweaks over time allowed a pressfield to retain atmosphere, provide security, and maintain an illumination schedule more or less standard to Yaodong's. They called this the Shadeshield.

The terraformers got to work almost immediately.

Now, a few hundred years later, most of the solar system was reaching population limits. Fervidia, uninhabitable due to its close proximity to the sun, was issued the most powerful Shadeshield in the system. Despite the old Solar League's best efforts, Fervidia proved to only be truly valuable as a manufacturing hub and industrial prison. Cerigo's ammonia-clouded skies, now crowded with decadent floating cities, looked down on a vast network of underground enclaves teeming with the less fortunate classes. Prahari, populated by some of the system's best and brightest artists, statesmen and academics, watched over old, dead Yaodong. And Hong Prime teemed with nearly a billion contracts, and a few hundred thousand citizens.

Out past the sparse pebbles of the Belt, the colony moons orbiting Albion and Cartesia known collectively as the Satellite Federation, now well on their feet and starting a population boom, kept a wary eye on their outward neighbors, the Frontier Territories. Life in the Frontier, in the distant worlds of the outer system, was only as good as the supply lines, and between the famines, plagues and chaos of their initial phases of colonization and their subsequent self-imposed exile from the rest of the system, people didn't exactly volunteer to live out in the Frontier these days. Overpopulation throughout the non-Frontier worlds of the system would become a serious issue within the next ten years, even after the significant casualties of the recent Sanzoku War. Really, Kwan thought, in a horrible way they'd been fortunate that the Roga was keeping the numbers down.

The Kiteri Roga was a terrible respiratory disorder which basically ensured that eighty percent of the system would never see their 70th birthday. It had cropped up about fifty years ago, around the same time ATMO5 first hit the market, though Hong Dominion's public relations machine had so far prevented the press from noticing that particular coincidence.

Before ATMO5, each brand of Shadeshield manufacturer had their own trade secret air formulas, their own proprietary technology.

Hong Dominion quietly bought out each of their competitors about sixty years back. They spent the next ten years standardizing the technology, and ATMO5 became the air everyone would breathe - until it eventually killed them.

Chen Chi-Wing, the current Chief Executive of Hong Dominion, had done a great job of building on the advances of his predecessors. He had expanded Hong's resource holdings in the Belt, headed up an R&D team to make some cosmetic improvements to Shadeshield sunrise and sunset capabilities, increased the number of contracts in their factories on Gushenxing to double production on those new, high-demand Shadeshield units, brought three new media companies under the Hong umbrella, and, while he wasn't able to break ATMO5 into the Frontier market during the Fringe War, he had used the war to secure Hong's monopoly among the League worlds. He was probably HD's best Chief Executive in a century.

Kwan Li smoked his stempipe and stared out at the sky, not so lost in thought that he would fail to notice as the Shadeshield jockeys painted tonight's sunset in every conceivable shade of red. Kwan had been sourced to be Chen's successor. He had spent his entire conscious life in the palace court; as a page, a trade negotiator, and planetary governor. Currently, he held the post of Representative for Hong in the Primary, the League of Worlds' governing body. One day, years from now, when the Chief Executive was ready to retire, the job would be Kwan's. He would accept the honor with thankfulness and grace, as did his predecessors.

But unlike his predecessors, who sought only to bring success to the coffers of Hong Dominion, Kwan saw the opportunity to make a difference on a larger scale. Even if it meant some changes for the company. Some short-term profit loss, as well, if his latest projections were to be believed.

He couldn't fix all of the issues facing the corporation, the League, or the system at large. But he had a few moves he could make that would improve a lot of lives, and put the corporation on a solid financial footing for the next few centuries.

Footsteps from the palace walk behind him broke his reverie. Two sets. They stopped behind him. Kwan did not turn around to acknowledge them; his visitor was expected.

"My lord," Chamberlain Fong announced in his usual grandiose manner, "The representative from Der Zweiwelten has arrived."

"Thank you, Chamberlain," the Dauphin replied. He patted the empty space on the bench next to him. "Come sit here, Darinka. Help me watch this gorgeous sunset."

The long, lean frame of Darinka Korovenko, Duchess Ravenscar, made its way around the bench, past Kwan, and found a seat on a rocky outcrop near the pool's small waterfall. The waterfall had been placed there specifically to create enough noise to foil attempts at clandestine audio recording. She patted the rock. "Thank you,

Dauphin, but here's metal more attractive. Besides, we wouldn't wish to fuel the fires of scandal, now, would we?"

They were a couple of young hotshot diplomats at the top of their game, and since they represented the two real economic powers in the inner system (the Prahari Republic kept their noses in their books), the press would frequently think of scenarios that might finally bring their two governments together. Der Zweiwelten was going to take over governmental administration of Hong's corporate territorial holdings. Hong Dominion would buy Fervidia outright from Der Zweiwelten. The Dauphin and the Duchess were both sex perverts secretly planning on getting "married" and birthing their own children like rutting animals, forming an archaic matrimonial alliance between the two governments and beginning a dynastic line that would rule the inner system for a thousand thousand years...

Neither Representative Korovenko nor Dauphin Kwan Li had any plans to start a dynastic line, or an archaic family unit of any kind. And even the idea of a live birth had, within the inner system at least, by now become the stuff of superstitious legend. But they were very much up to something, and since they were too much in the public eye to avoid all scrutiny, they figured they may as well lean into the rumor mill. A bit.

Hence their secret meeting - in the open air, on top of the largest mountain in the system, in full view to about half a billion of Hong's citizens and contracts, should they look up at the Palace with their macrobinoculars (as they often did).

"Fair enough," said Kwan. "Have you heard about Kepler?"

Korovenko nodded. "It's just the first. Stringfellow's got his hooks in just about every governor's mouth."

"You have proof of that, by chance?"

She frowned, crossed her arms. "As if that matters. He's recently caught the ear of my illustrious sister, by the way."

"And I am sure he's pouring poison directly into it. How is Her Highness the Baroness?"

"Pigheaded as ever. Still threatened by my mere existence. She sends her regards, by the way. But I had an idea about how we might be able to use this Federation situation to our advantage."

Kwan took a long drag from his stempipe. He knew where this was going. "Who do you want to bring in?"

"Pellas?" she ventured. "We're going to need a ship and a crew, and we couldn't use any of ours, even if we had any. The *Pangolin* would suit our needs."

"Pellas." It wasn't the worst idea. "Stateless status might be good for deniability." He nodded. The symbolism involved in using the *Pangolin* was especially compelling. "He will have to go through Vanakar, though."

"She's a professional."

"I had someone I wanted to bring in, as well." He wasn't looking forward to this part of the conversation.

"Who is it?"

"Okwende."

"*Der mist*...he can't know. The whole point is that if this breaks down, he's protected."

"It is time, we will need him-"

"We don't know that." She stood up, smoothed out her skirt, and started pacing. "It could take decades before we see any real results."

"We have plenty of telemetry data already, it should not take long to get something workable."

"The war pushed up our timetable more than I'm comfortable with. Presentation-wise, we wouldn't be at our best. Would you really be comfortable taking this to your Board?"

"Of course. The Board would not like it though, the profitability curve is far outside their lead limits."

She stopped pacing, and stared him down. "I'm serious, Li."

"So am I. Okwende is out there making decisions without any idea what is happening. We need to get him on board before he makes any policy decisions that hold the plan back."

"If there's anyone left to make policy before Stringfellow puts everyone in his pocket."

"We need to tell him, Darinka."

She nodded. "So, Pellas, Okwende..." She looked up. "Chamberlain?"

Chamberlain Fong approached from the palace portico. "Apologies for the interruption, but dinner will now be served in the Avalon Dining Room."

Kwan got up from his bench. "Thank you, Chamberlain. We will be there presently."

After Fong had returned inside, Darinka shook her head. "Fong still creeps me out. He's so...old."

"They say he has served the Chief Executive's household for over a hundred years, but I would bet he is not nearly as old as he looks."

"He doesn't look a day under a hundred and fifty to me."

"Anything is possible." He sat back down on the bench, patted the space next to him again. "Come on, there's only a few minutes of sunset left. Let's give the people what they want."

Inside the Palace, Chamberlain Fong walked the cool, open breezeways, taking in the relatively fresh air in the early evening. Running the Executive's household was a task that kept him busy for nearly every waking moment, but his time from evening meal to bedtime was usually reserved as a time for quiet and reflection. Fong stopped at a railing, the view facing down onto the expansive Infinite City below. A pair of contracts passed behind him, no doubt on their way to tend to the guests in the lounge. The city below him, and indeed the whole Hong Dominion Corporation, was as strong as it had ever been. Its inter-economy was in fine shape, the people were content; the needs (and most wants) of even Hong's contracts were well cared for. Executive Chen Chi-Wing, tenth Chairman of the Board, was second only to the legendary Xing himself in wisdom and power.

Fong was indeed over 100 years old; well over, in fact. There was a perfectly logical explanation for this, though no one in the court had ever suspected it. It never seemed to raise suspicion that Fong outlived everyone; the court accepted it, and that was enough. The Chamberlain was a confidant, a keeper of secrets, and an agent of disinformation and subterfuge. He was loyal to only one, the Executive; any and all that threatened that office would meet his steel. And the Chamberlain's main concern, as he watched the dust devils dance in the quiet evening streets, was the quality of the laundry.

The Executive's linens had returned with a peculiar scent to them, one not unpleasant, but that was not the point. They carried the scent of lavender instead of Calypsan jasmine, as the linens were required to smell. An inspection of the laundry had turned up nothing out of spec, there was no opportunity for error at any point in the process. The folding rooms were spotless, the laundry transports hermetically sealed, and yet...

In the end, it was a training error; a new contract, a Disa, hadn't been given a few necessary engrams for laundry tasks. Fong had spoken with the supervisor in charge, and the matter was put to rest. And yet...

Chamberlain Fong passed the Cypress Garden, where he found Executive Chen eating a bowl of Hadro-Bits. Chen had only that day returned from being guest of honor at an economic trend conference at Prahari's Cernan University. Chen sat, entranced, on a cushion as he compared the figures on his datapad with those on a holoimager in front of him. The latest news was vexing; Lord Renner had just bought out Cinderbuilt, last of the cultured wood manufacturers. Various Houses of Der Zweiwelten had spent the last five years buying up and shutting down all the producers, likely in an effort to inflate the price of both real and cultured wood. That the oligarchs were once again toying with market forces wasn't the vexing part; Chen simply couldn't seem to suss out their long-term strategy. Wood - cultured or otherwise - was hardly a consumer commodity, rare as it was. "Good evening, my friend," Chen said, glad of any distraction. "All is well?"

The sky was now a peculiar shade of dark maroon, one that Fong had to admit he had not seen from the Hong Prime sky in all his years. He would have to compliment the Shadeshield jockeys, artisans in their field. "Indeed, my lord. I have observed dust devils along the south wall. It will be good sleeping weather tonight."

There was a long pause. "I wonder," probed Chen, "how is the Dauphin this evening?"

Fong responded truthfully, if diplomatically. "The Executive would be keenly interested in the report of the minutes of the Primary's latest session." In truth, Chen was livid over the Kepler Rebellion, as the press was beginning to call it, and despite Li and Korovenko's best efforts, the situation had not improved. Whether their cloak-and-dagger plotting - whatever it was - would solve the issue remained to be seen. Chen allowed the two a wide berth of operation, for now; but at the first sign that the Duchess was somehow using the Dauphin, Hong and Der Zweiwelten would be back at each other's throats. A new Hong Defense Fleet had been fast-tracked for exactly that possibility; a fact Chen had made sure Li was unaware of.

Chen sighed. "I fear my heir has an incomplete understanding of intersystem politics. He has concentrated for too long on the interests of Hong Dominion; it is but a stone in a large pool."

"My lord, with respect, it is the Executive's role to concentrate on his empire because it is his empire. Zhang line 74 tells one and all, 'How will you clothe your neighbor's wife and your own on one man's salary?'" This brought a chuckle from Chen. "He will make a fine Executive when the time comes, and from what I have seen his diplomatic skills continue to improve."

"Hmm," Chen considered this. Finally, he laughed heartily. "Chamberlain Fong, you are indeed wise beyond even your years. Thank you for both advising and amusing me today. As days go, this has been a long one and I shall be glad to see it finished."

Fong took that as a dismissal. He stood and bowed. "My lord, may your evening be pleasant. As in the past, if you were to require anything..."

"Thank you, Chamberlain," Chen replied with a slight nod, and returned to his oligarchs and Hadro-Bits. Fong left to retire for the evening.

Fong dismissed the problems of the day from his mind. The time for worry was past - now it was dusk, time for reflection. But the unease could not be shaken. It was beyond the laundry problem, beyond Kepler; something was scratching at his mind, something he couldn't pinpoint. It was as if he were standing in an empty room, but couldn't shake the feeling that someone was standing behind him, watching over his shoulder.

The War was over. There were a few bumps in the Primary, but that's always to be expected. Overall, everything was going well for Hong Dominion.

Fong was well over a hundred years old, which was long enough to know that "everything is going well" is a likely time for the wheels to fall off completely.

4

PRIMARY HALL • LAIKA STATION • YAODONG ORBIT

"That is a deliberate obscuring of the truth, and you know it!" Castor Pellas was uncharacteristically flustered. His face was red, his hair a frenzied mess. The Frontier had gone too far this time. "The Federation has never intruded on the sovereignty-"

Speaker Okwende sounded the quiet alert. "We will have order in these proceedings. Would the honorable representative from the Satellite Federation please be seated until it is once again his turn to speak. The envoy from the Frontier Territories may continue. Mr. Stringfellow?"

Clyde Stringfellow, who felt, as always, that he would be more comfortably addressed as the envoy of the Kintsugi Nation's than the Frontier's (a very tired procedural argument in the Primary), smiled a Cheshire Cat grin at Pellas, looked down at his notes, then sighed. "Thank you, Presiding Speaker. Despite the protestations of the Federation's honorable representative, there is a wealth of evidence to support these claims. Which I will present to you today, without interruption as Representative Pellas pleases."

"May I remind the envoy that he is present here at the Primary's pleasure, and if he wishes to continue to maintain this goodwill, he will refrain from baiting the representatives and please adhere to the facts," Speaker Okwende replied, not at all entertained by the envoy's tactics. A representative stood up. "The Primary recognizes a brief statement from the Prahari Representative. Ms. Cross?"

"Thank you, Presiding Speaker. The Prahari Republic would remind the visiting observer from the Frontier to outline the matter at hand, rather than simply point fingers at the representative from the Satellite Federation."

"The honorable Ms. Cross is reminded," replied Stringfellow, "that the actions of the Satellite Federation are indeed the matter at hand, as they have caused this situation in the first place."

"So is it the intent of all these sovereign moons of Albion and Cartesia to each send their own representative here to the Primary?" Cross asked innocently.

"I fail to see the importance of this detail to an already autonomous lunar government," Stringfellow smiled incredulously. "Of all these representatives, I would have assumed that the Prahari Republic would be sympathetic to their plight."

"Oh, I've taken no side in this matter. My concern is merely that, if we're to have half a hundred more worlds in the Primary, Laika Station will be too small a venue. I'd like to get started on a new facility." This brought a wave of polite laughter from the representatives and their subordinates, deflating the tension somewhat, except for the Frontier and the Satellite Federation. The stakes were far too high for them to take things at all lightly. "However, if I may address the continued remarks of the honorable envoy of the Frontier Territories, why have the individual members of these newly sovereign worlds not sent representatives themselves?" Representative Cross kept her line of questioning light, hoping not to be interrupted before her endgame could make it to the floor. "Or is it that they would prefer to allow the Frontier to speak for them in perpetuity?"

The question hung like humidity in the air. The Primary Chamber was completely silent. Wilma Cross of Prahari knew exactly what she was doing by asking that question. The same series of questions had danced, unspoken, in the head of everyone in the chamber, if not the entire system.

A surprising figure stood to break the silence. The Dauphin Kwan of Hong Dominion, stood. "Presiding Speaker, if I may say a few words..."

Speaker Okwende obliged him, thankful for an end to the painful silence. "You may. The Primary recognizes the Dauphin Kwan Li of the Hong Dominion Corporation."

The Dauphin addressed the Primary, unlit stempipe in hand. "Thank you, Speaker. This development is distressing to my people. Not since the earliest of the Colonial Wars have any of Hong's holdings expressed the least displeasure with their ruling government. For this revolution to take hold on so many worlds at once is...curious. The Executive is acutely concerned. And while the esteemed envoy from the Frontier has pointed out a number of what I would consider to be minor flaws in representation and governance-"

"Minor? You consider the conditional taxation-"

Okwende sounded the quiet alarm again, with a relish that did not go unnoticed. "The envoy from the Frontier will take care to observe proper courtesy. Continue, Dauphin."

"Thank you, Speaker." Kwan continued. "As I was saying, while there are a number of small representational difficulties between the Satellite Federation and its constituents, I can say with perfect confidence that such a situation would not have occurred on, say, the moons of Hong Prime, during their time. Or some of our current colonies in the Belt. Have any of you visited these places? Poverty means silver plating instead of gold. Hong treats its colonies like an extension of the ruling planet itself. Since the settlement of Hong Prime, the Hong Dominion Corporation has believed - and still believes - that any territorial holdings are an inseparable part of the Hong corporate empire.

"While there is no governance on the gas giants that the worlds of the Federation orbit, that merely puts them all on the most equal footing. Surely these moons can see that they would be stronger-"

"Thank you for your input, Dauphin," Stringfellow said. "I can see that the Primary is not interested in the plight of the people of the Satellite Federation. I will now return to the Kintsugi Nation and relay your words to my Okaasan Heika. It remains to be seen if She will grant asylum to any of those who are suffering under the yoke of such tyranny." With that, he gathered his notes and exited the chamber in a huff.

After a long silence, Kwan, still standing, put down his pipe. "Ah, motion to recess?" he ventured.

"Seconded," said Der Zweiwelten representative Korovenko.

"Carried," said Speaker Lysander Okwende, with clear relief. "A two-hour recess is in order. Enjoy your lunch."

As the diplomatic teams gathered their belongings, Korovenko approached the Speaker's dais. "Speaker, may I meet with you in chambers for a moment?"

"I'm going for lunch. Off the clock, as it were. Be in my chambers in one hour."

"But Speaker-"

"Enjoy your lunch!"

Fifty-nine minutes later, Representatives Kwan and Korovenko waited outside the Speaker's chambers.

Speaker Lysander Okwende arrived, carrying a sandwich almost as big as his head. "The line at the commissary was atrocious. Can you believe they make me wait in the line like everyone else?" The speaker got no reaction from the representatives. He sighed. "Come in, children. Watch me eat this sandwich, then ruin my day with whatever it is you have."

They entered his chambers.

Laika Station was known for its genuine wood interiors, and Okwende's chambers were no exception. Floors, ceiling, wall paneling, shelving, furniture - the entire room was made of wood. His desk was an old statesman's desk from Yaodong; Kwan remembered it was called a Resolute Desk. The view of Yaodong from the window behind Okwende's desk distracted Kwan every time he'd been in the room. The yellowish-green pearl hung in space like a poisoned grape. Okwende gestured for them to sit in two cavernous chairs appointed in very soft cowskin leather. Everything in the room dated from before the Noble Egress, including, as Okwende explained, the recipe for his sandwich.

"Children," Okwende began (Okwende was only about 15 years older than themselves, so his use of "children" here was more patronizing than anything), "this is called a Dagwood. It is the best sandwich ever made. Okaasan Heika herself could not have devised such a perfect sandwich." Okwende ate the sandwich, big as it was, in seven large bites. The sarcastic swipe at the Frontier's fictional figurehead goddess-ruler did not go unnoticed by the two young representatives.

"Now," he said, as he savored his last bite, "tell me what it is you two have been up to. Wait!" he stopped Darinka before she could even begin her spiel. "Are you behind the revolutions in the Satellite Federation?"

"What? No!" Kwan replied.

"All right then. What is it you want to talk to me about?" Okwende dabbed at his multi-colored sweater, where an errant drop of mayonnaise had landed.

Darinka Korovenko and Kwan Li were quite literally born and bred to be where they were at this moment. They were brilliant leaders of their respective peoples on an interplanetary stage of high-stakes statecraft. But even they were intimidated by Lysander Okwende, a man who could idly wipe condiments off his shirt while maintaining the poise and dignity expected of the greatest statesman of his time.

He looked at each of them. "You have forty-seven minutes."

"The human race has less than 100 years left to live," Kwan blurted out. This was rather uncharacteristic of him; he was quite nervous.

Okwende considered this. He slowly stood up, walked over to his sideboard, poured himself a glass of Orkney Style Reserve Cask, added a single cooling marble, and brought it back to his desk. He sat back in his chair. "Why don't you begin at the beginning."

"ATMO5 is basically the only thing keeping the human race alive at this point," Darinka began. "But it has side effects."

Okwende had heard the tales. "There are old stories and superstitions about artificial atmospheres preventing people from, I don't know, growing babies inside them or whatever. We've got consulting clinics now, we don't have to worry about," he waved dismissively, "animal husbandry."

"It's beyond that, I am afraid," said Kwan, willing to skip past yet another harmful side effect. "The Corporation would never publicly admit this, but ATMO5 is causing the Roga. And it will get worse.

Future generations will have shorter life expectancies. Within 100 years, no one will live past the age of ten."

"Not to mention the ever-present threat that the Sanzoku might return to complete their sweep of the system," Darinka added.

"As we see it, there are two choices: lift Emerson-Paek, or restore Operation Second Egress."

Okwende drank his entire glass in one pull. "Please tell me you're not building a secret army of intelligent robots to steward generations of a human race of ten-year-olds until they can figure a way out of this."

Kwan was once again distracted by the ruined Yaodong outside Okwende's office window. "No, the Emerson-Paek Act...needs to be kept intact. No high-intelligence processors. We, ah," he glanced at Darinka for moral support, "we may have resurrected Second Egress."

Okwende was not pleased. "We put a stop to Second Egress because we signed the Treaty of Kambei. We can't cross Frontier space without permission. We're lucky they never found out about the Iditarod probes."

"But those probes are still broadcasting telemetry," Darinka said. "Good telemetry. Potentially habitable worlds, with natural, breathable atmospheres."

Okwende gritted his teeth. "Potentially. And who's going out there to find these habitable worlds? In what craft? May I remind you that the Coalition fleet was decimated. I'm sure everyone has their shipyards working around the clock, but there's nothing close to ready."

"We're working on that. We've spoken to Federation Admiral Vanakar, she's offered us her cooperation for however long she's still in command of anything."

If anyone else had come to him with this, he'd have tossed them out an airlock. Figuratively. "That might be useful, when the time comes." Okwende was beginning to settle into the idea. He leaned forward conspiratorially. "A ship from the Federation wouldn't be able to violate Kambei once the Federation doesn't exist."

"I also have a Hong subsidiary who is very close to perfecting an ultra-FTL drive," Kwan said. "They should have a prototype within the month."

Okwende sat back again. "And one day your prototype will just disappear?"

Kwan allowed himself the ghost of a smile. "Belt Pirates are not just a thing from old stories, Speaker."

Okwende flashed him a disapproving look. "As you well know." He shook his head. "This is an awful risk. But, if you're right about ATMO5, it may be a necessary one. We just have to make sure the Frontier doesn't get wind of any of this."

Korovenko and Kwan looked at each other, agreed that that was that, and slowly extracted themselves from their cavernous chairs.

"One more thing." They turned back to Okwende, now standing behind his desk. "You could have done all this behind my back. Why come to me now?"

"Speaker," Darinka said, "everything that happens under your administration is your responsibility. You would have been on the hook for it if it failed, whether you knew about it or not."

"And if it succeeds, which it will," pointed out Kwan, "it will be you who oversaw the rescue of the human race from certain oblivion. Twice, counting the Sanzoku War. Your legacy will be assured."

"Children," said Speaker Okwende, "I think there's more than enough legacy to go around. Go, save humanity."

5

THE THISTLE & BROOM PUBLIC HOUSE · ENGELSTADT · CERIGO · DER ZWEIWELTEN

The Thistle & Broom was one of those dive bars: the kind where your feet stick to the floor, the screens only show boot rugby games (at maximum volume), and the clientele are not exactly the most talkative. Lone men and women, mostly expat-Tigers from the Fed or the occasional hayseed Frontier escapee, occupied a handful of booths and tables waiting for Stadt Flight Control to grant them a launch window, or for the arrival of their special someone. Here, that special someone could be their dealer, their contact, their fare, their mark, maybe even their spaceport mechanic with the bad news on a drive repair.

A young woman strode confidently through the doorway. The bouncer (this was Engelstadt, after all; there had to be some kind of security) started after her, but stopped short when he saw the winged V on the back of her stegskin bomber jacket. He subconsciously clutched his recently-healed right thumb in his left hand as he remembered the last time she was here, and he had tried to ID her.

It had not gone well for the bouncer. Or the bartender, several patrons, or the Thistle's glassware budget.

The bouncer tapped his earpiece. "Yes?" a tinny, entitled-sounding, Hyperion-accented voice replied.

"Cassini."

"I understand. I'll be out in a few moments. Do keep an eye out, won't you?"

"Da."

The woman in the stegskin jacket sat at the bar, at the opposite end from a few girls who were bored out of their minds waiting for a wet-behind-the-ears Frontier mark to start their meters. The bartender polished a glass stereotypically as he addressed his latest customer in a rather charming Caledonian brogue.

"What'll it be?"

"Where's Magnus?"

"Still in traction, thanks to you," the barkeep replied with a smile as he sauntered over. "Should we call the gendarmes now, or after you break a chair over another poor bastard's head?"

"Look, I was here for a business meeting. How was I supposed to know it was gonna end like that?"

"You here for another business meeting?"

"In a few minutes. Hopefully less eventful. Laika Tonic."

"Yes, ma'am." The bartender set down the polished glass and strode off to prepare her drink. From seemingly nowhere, an impeccably-dressed man appeared at her side, his back to the bar, watching his customers.

"You know, every time you walk through that door my insurance premiums go absolutely sky high. I adore it all the same."

"Hello, Desmond. Still slumming it in this third-rate trashbarge of a town?"

"It's the life of kings, my darling. Absolutely the life of kings."

"That's one way to put it." The bartender arrived with two bottles, poured the vodka and tonic into her glass simultaneously, then produced a moonfruit wedge from his apron pouch and garnished the drink. It was one of those dive bars.

Desmond got serious for a moment. "I did say I was sorry about Mr. Gunther. I understand your instincts, but I do hope in the future you'll reserve your patented berserker rage exclusively for those who deserve it, and limit-" he looked at the bar surrounding them, "the collateral damage." He ran a hand through his slicked-back blond hair, then brushed a bit of dandruff from his shoulder. "Since you're here, I assume you're interested in the job."

"I'd like to hear more about it. I'm doubling my usual fee, though." She took a sip of her Laika tonic. "The latest embargo complicates things. Other than that, the usual rules apply."

Desmond grimaced. "Yes, well, I think in this case there might be a bit of bending of the rules in order. There's a passenger who needs to accompany the cargo, I'm afraid. It's not up for negotiation, something about keeping tabs on the condition of the cargo."

"I did cryo hauling once, never again. Rule Number One, never transport anything that's alive. That includes passengers – they're more trouble than they're worth."

"No, no, no, it's not cryo pods or anything like that. This guy's got some kind of volatile medicines, temperature and magnetic-sensitive."

"And he can't fly it out himself?"

"Not all of us were born in a cockpit, Cass. To be precise, his pilot got pinched by the gendarmes yesterday. A spot of permit trouble, I gather. Why don't you go talk to him about it, he's right over there." Desmond nodded, indicating a sweaty, uncomfortable-looking man nursing a needlenose gimlet in the most private booth in the place.

"You'd better be right about this one, Des."

He took a sip of her drink. "All I ask is your usual undying affection...and, of course, my usual ten percent." Cassini rolled her eyes at him as she started toward the booth. "Cass," he called after her, "do go easy on the furniture this time."

Cassini sat across from the sweaty man, who looked, for all the world, like a 17-year-old about to buy a bottle of Caledonian whisky with a spoofed dermal chip. Her current ship, the *Portia*, was in dire need of repairs. Also, it had been impounded on Hibernia over some licensing...irregularities, meaning she was reduced to offering only her piloting services. As it turns out, not a lot of people need a pilot without a ship, so pickings were slim. Doing a courier run for an easy mark like this guy would probably net her double her rate, even beyond the double she was already tacking on for breaking embargo.

"Hey."

"Oh. Um, hello. Are you...can you..."

"Yeah, probably. Tell me about the job."

The sweaty man wiped his brow with an already damp shirt sleeve, slightly displacing the cheap wig he was wearing. It made her realize that he somehow looked familiar, in a way she couldn't immediately place. "Well, it's..." He looked around the bar, making sure no one was listening, watching, or lip-reading. He leaned in. "Do you know about the latest round of Caspian flu that's going around on Kyuzo?"

"Not really." She'd spent the last few days trying to drum up work down in Mullvagrad, where intersystem news takes a back seat to news of the "which petty criminal double-crossed which somewhat less petty criminal and then got stabbed in the face for his or her troubles" variety.

"Well, this Caspian flu, it's, you know, it's really bad, and until a few days ago I worked for Trevalya. They wanted to charge a lot for this vaccine, drafonitol, and I didn't think that was right...so I stole it. And quit."

"Do they know you stole the vaccine?"

"Not yet," he replied, sheepishly. "But eventually, they're going to notice they don't have any drafonitol to overcharge for."

If she kept him talking just a few minutes longer, she'd figure out how she knew him. "How much did you steal?"

"16 kilos. Enough to inoculate probably half the uninfected population, but I can also unlock the peptide copy protection..."

As he droned on, she also thought about the modifiers this job presented. Standard rate x distance: 70,000 darics (if Cerigo to Kyuzo). Risk of border/trade embargo violation: + 70,000 darics. Dangerous cargo: + 50,000. Mark tax: + another 50k. Flying an unfamiliar ship...

"Des told me you'd already hired someone for this?"

"Yes. A woman named Kellar? She had a problem with her licenses when she got here."

"Ugh, Kellar. Ship licenses?"

"No, no, no. I guess she had some pilot's licenses that weren't renewed, or maybe they were fake, I don't know."

Probably all of the above, knowing Esme Kellar. And while Cass had never been on Esme's ship, the SS *Featherstone*, she just knew it was a toilet.

"Her ship is in impound?"

"Yes, but the man at the impound office said he'd let me have it for a thousand krona, so that's no problem."

The least surprising thing he'd said in the two minutes they'd known each other. If you had enough krona, the sky was the limit on Cerigo.

"Well, I don't deal in krona, I only take League darics, and right now I'm looking at a 750,000-daric job. And I don't negotiate. That's my offer."

"I'm on a humanitarian mission-"

Cards on the table. "You're Vik Engstrom, the recently disgraced chief operations officer of one of the largest independent pharmaceutical companies in the inner system. I think you're good for it."

"What?! I will have you know-"

"Look, the wig is terrible. And I just spent the last few days in Mullvagrad, where your little secret made a lot of waves. Plenty of people down there have, or had, family at Dom Vauban. Not big fans of the little prison testing lab you set up there on the backs of their people. Let's not pretend that this is anything more than a new start for you in the Frontier, paid for with your drafonitol."

While he was still a sweaty bundle of nerves, Engstrom seemed to suddenly regrow a (thin) backbone.

"750,000. That's...an awful lot."

"I guess it depends on how badly you want to leave the civilized system." She passed him a cocktail napkin, on which she had written a series of numbers and letters. "As soon as I have 750,000 darics in this account, the people of Kyuzo are as good as cured. Or, you know, whatever."

Engelstadt was one of the older floating communities, or stadts, of Cerigo. When the planet was originally colonized, everyone lived in underground cities like Mullvagrad. Those carved-out cave cities descended into dens of iniquity once the floating platforms were established and the rich could finally take their place with the storm dragons in the rarefied air of Cerigo's yellow-tinted atmosphere.

Fast-forward enough decades, however, and what was once high-end is now yesterday's news – bad enough when you're talking about transports or computing systems, but at the scale of a floating metropolis (or thirty), it can threaten a planet's economy.

Der Zweiwelten solved this by giving each city a purpose. Tourism, entertainment, trade, industry. There was a city to fill every municipal niche. Even a secondary spaceport for overflow traffic that the main port on Kikotostadt didn't have the space (or the time, or the inclination) to take on. Beyond its role as a tertiary spaceport, Engelstadt also had a good amount of open space once half the population had left for a newer stadt, which meant that there was plenty of space for one of the largest impound lots on the planet. And plenty of space for a single ship to get lost in the shuffle.

Cass' trip to the Engelstadt impound was short. The clerk was indeed on the take, and the *Featherstone* was as much of a toilet as she expected. Within about ten minutes, they were breaking orbit from Cerigo.

The *Featherstone* was a typical quarter-sized commercial cargo hauler: it was underpowered, over-engineered, and smelled like ferrometic acid, which is what Kellar had been regularly hauling (and, apparently, unsuccessfully unloading, judging by the deck stains) for the last year or so, in between other hires. There was trash, dirty clothing, and decomposing food waste all over the ship.

Engstrom wandered the ship in disgusted wonder, holding a handkerchief to his nose and mouth. He poked his head into the cockpit. "This place really is a toilet. Is it better or worse than the last time you were here?"

"I've never been on this ship before."

"But you knew exactly how to run it–"

"It's a Nikolishin *Zephyr 5*. It's not hard."

"Then how'd you know this place would be so disgusting?"

"Are you writing a book?"

"No. No, I'm sorry. I'll just, um, leave you to it." He turned to go to the hold, where he could check on his cases of vaccine – given enough distance, it was the only guarantee he had against a sure exports conviction in the Zweiwelten courts. Best to let the pilot do her job.

"I don't know Kellar that well," she called after him without turning from her readouts, "but I know her well enough."

Kellar was definitely a pig, but at least the ship wasn't falling apart. Engstrom certainly wasn't going to want to keep the *Featherstone*, and Cassini figured she might be able to squeeze another 50,000 darics (or whatever exchangeable currency they use out there) out of some desperate Frontier refugee-in-waiting. Between the earnings from this trip, the sale of the *Featherstone*, and her various savings, she might finally have enough saved to fix up a heavy freighter she happened to know was gathering rust in a lonely corner of Peng's Space Salvage, out in the Belt. With essentially all of the merchant fleet pressed into government supply transport and patrol duty, the market for independent large-capacity cargo hauling was basically wide open. The governments of the League had their shipyards running continuous shifts to crank out new fleets as soon as possible, but it would be a good six months at least before the first of them would be ready.

She could have that junker ready to go in one month, easy. Given another two to three months on the open market, she could have the independent heavy hauler industry basically cornered. Contract more ships as they become available, and it wouldn't be long before she had a medium-sized shipping empire on her hands.

If she could pull off this job without getting pinched.

6

ASTEROID CX489G673 (now redacted) • THE BELT TERRITORIES

There was a whole lot of space between Cerigo and Kyuzo, and once you got past the Belt the risk of running into the MOE increased exponentially.

The Ministry of Export had patrols on every axis on the Federation's side of the Kambei Line, the imaginary border between the League of Worlds and the Kintsugi Nation. As long as the Nation (or the "Frontier Territories," as League officials had insisted on calling it for the past hundred years) refused to officially join the League, the MOE would enforce economic sanctions against it. Ask any League bureaucrat and they'd tell you these sanctions were in place to prevent the Territories from becoming a military threat. Ask any citizen of the Nation and they'd tell you that the League was trying to choke them out of existence.

None of this mattered to Cassini, though. Which goods were under normal embargo versus which goods were X9 (being caught transporting X9 items meant an automatic trip to Dom Vauban, the barrel for all the League's bad apples), and how much the Frontier would pay to get a hold of embargoed goods – those were the relevant facts.

On a more operational level, for those in Cassini's field of extra-legal transport, there was some concern in Cassini's line of work about how to bypass the MOE patrols. A few things were on the smugglers' side: the absolute vastness of space in the area in question, the limited number of ships the League had to patrol the area, and the fact that no bureaucracy is completely immune to bribery. The League, however, countered these shortcomings by deploying a series of automated sensor buoys surrounding the system at the Kambei Line, and the patrols merely had to monitor the buoys and deploy more of them to problem areas as necessary.

For Cassini and her colleagues, the answer to this problem was Bob.

The asteroid was quite small, but its unique curvature and irregular surface allowed her to set down the Featherstone on a small landing pad near a ramshackle building. Other than those two features, the asteroid was just another lump of ore in space.

As Engstrom poked his head outside, he tasted the thin air and felt the lightness of the gravity. The rock's shadeshield was probably one of the older Yang-Yeovils, made for very small-scale applications. "This doesn't look like Kyuzo to me," he said. "Is this...some kind of very poorly run refueling station?"

Cassini gave him a withering stare. "Stay on the ship. I'll only be a minute." As he reluctantly shut the hatch, she started toward the building. In a previous life, this asteroid had, in fact, been a refueling station for a band of Belt pirates back in the romantic, heady days of colonization. Bob had kept the landing pad, dismantled and removed the fueling apparatus, and set up shop here. The advantage of this particular rock, for Bob, was that it contained a rare combination of ores that were resistant to most sensors. Also, he'd taken the liberty of decharting the asteroid from the League's map databases.

Most importantly, the relative underside of the asteroid just happened to be in an excellent location to intercept the Kambei Line buoy network's plexus signal – the signal that collected all buoy data to relay back to MOE headquarters back on Laika Station. Bob had data on every ship that crossed the line, buoy maintenance schedules, patrol assignments, inter-departmental communications. If you needed to find a hole in the buoy network, Bob was your guy. If a ship in your organization got pinched, Bob could point you to which officers could make the whole thing quietly go away. It also didn't hurt that Bob used to be an export officer himself, so he knew all the protocols. Bob was a gift for anyone in the business, and Cass was one of a handful of people who even knew how to find this place.

Bob didn't know Cass was coming, but that was standard procedure. *I will never converse with a client over any communications system – I do all business face-to-face. If there's already a ship on the landing pad, wait your turn. When you get to the shack, press the intercom. The door will open, you sit in the waiting room until I come for you.* This was the way Bob wanted it, so one tended not to balk all that much.

Cass reached Bob's shack – actually a large, two-storey building – and pressed the intercom. After a brief pause, there was a grinding sound from the airlock mechanism and the door opened slightly. She stepped through, into the waiting room.

The waiting room was sparsely appointed, with threadbare cushioned chairs and an image of an old Colonial-era pirate ship hanging slightly askew on one of the walls. There were more than a few spiderwebs in whatever nooks and crannies the spiders found strategic. This was typical; Bob wasn't one for cleaning up.

The door to Bob's office was open.

This was not typical.

Cass produced her pistol, though she wasn't even sure if it still worked. When had she last charged the cells? If anything was awry, she hoped it might give an opponent pause if they saw that she was armed.

Gingerly, she entered through the partially-open office door. Bob's desk was a complete mess, but again, that was normal. There were images of his family: his wife, lost to the Roga about ten years ago; and two sons, one lost at Newtonia during the War last year, and the other now at university on Kepler. Everything looked completely normal, except for one thing – the distinct lack of Bob.

She searched the rest of the building. Much of it was unused, but based on the makeshift bedroom and kitchen she could tell that Bob had made this his home, which made her sad. For some reason, she'd had the idea that his "office" was his day job, that at the end of every day he would fly home to some conapt on Persephone or wherever. She decided to head back to the ship, once she tried the server room. She pressed the door release button. The door slowly opened. She barely had time to bring her pistol to bear.

"May I help you?" a man calmly asked in a gratingly posh Hyperion accent.

The man was tall and thin, his menacing air reinforced by his vaguely fascist black overcoat. The uniform of the League's Special Services. He easily snatched the pistol from her hands, and threw it over his shoulder. She watched as another Special walking by behind him caught the pistol without looking and kept going, not even breaking step. There was, in fact, a whole flurry of activity happening behind the man: Special agents removing drives and other equipment from what appeared to be Bob's communication interception nerve center.

"Where's Bob?" was about all she could manage, under the circumstances.

The man smiled, and Cass wished he hadn't. It made her imagine that somewhere there was a long list of people for whom that smile was the last thing they would ever see, and she hoped her name wasn't on it. "Mr. Andiamo is being detained for a series of crimes against the state. May I ask what you're doing here, Miss?"

She smiled sheepishly. "Leaving?" She turned and ran. Neither the Special agent nor his team gave chase, the agent at the door simply gave a series of orders in a calm tone, which unnerved her even more. Since she was heading in the opposite direction she couldn't hear his orders specifically, but something told her it would take a miracle for her to get out of this one. She made it to the waiting room, and through the airlock door.

It was the heat that hit her first, followed closely by the burning smell.

They were careful not to hit the drive section, since the *Featherstone* was in atmosphere, but the bulk of the ship was a burning cinder. Small fireballs erupted as gaseous systems let out the last of their supply. Tears ran down her face - more from the irritants in the air stinging her eyes than anything else, she told herself.

"Miss?"

The Special agent was at the airlock door.

"Miss, we have a number of questions we'd like to ask."

7 |

CELL #KL-09542 • DOM VAUBAN • FERVIDIA • DER ZWEIWELTEN

There was no trial.

In the end, for most of those who were aware of the situation, the whole thing was considered to be a hugely efficient exercise in judicial management and bureaucratic cooperation.

As a Federation citizen, Cassini Green had initially been assigned a Public Advocate, a tweedy little man named Berthold Donskoi, who had advised her on her few legal options. He'd told her that they had used an experimental machine on Bob to extract information regarding the criminal organizations who used his services. It was unclear as to the accuracy of the information obtained, but Cass didn't recognize the names of any of the people indicted using Bob's "extracted" testimony. As for Bob himself, he was never charged with any crimes - but he was never officially released, either, which Cass found disconcerting. She hoped it meant he was off on a witness protection pleasure cruise, and not in an incinerator.

Der Zweiwelten's representatives were very pleased that Viktor Engstrom was stopped before he could make it to Kyuzo. They were somewhat displeased when they discovered that the drafonitol was destroyed in the action, but "such is the price of justice," said their counsel. No comment was made regarding any ongoing plague on Kyuzo, or the actual condition of the population there.

Cass herself was subsequently remanded to the custody of the League, at which point she had lost her Advocate. The League chose, due to the overwhelming evidence against her, to skip straight to sentencing. Ten years in Dom Vauban didn't sound too bad, really, unless you factor in the fact that the average prisoner lasts less than a year there.

Fervidia had the strongest shadeshield in the system, powerful enough to protect against solar flares and keep the temperature just barely tolerable for humans. The Dom had the system's largest smelting operation - even larger than Caldera - and like its adjoining shipyard and other factories, was completely run with prison labor. There were also the usual liberties being taken by those who ran the facility; black markets, human trafficking, controlled substances. It was, in short, one of the least pleasant places in the system.

Cass had made up her mind to make it through the full ten years of her sentence. Sitting in her darkened cell five months in, she had yet to even make it into general population.

She'd started off strong by commandeering the transport craft bringing her and the rest of the latest crop of convicts to the Dom. She crashed the small craft through the transport control tower, barely landed it without killing everyone aboard, and assembled a group from among the less injured to hijack an outgoing shuttle. Unfortunately, the only shuttle that was available hadn't yet been refueled, and thus the convicts' revolution Cass had fomented did not succeed. She was placed in solitary confinement indefinitely, which all parties involved agreed was probably the best move.

They had put her in a very small cell, barely tall enough to stand in. A food paste dispenser hung off the side wall, near the door. There was a toilet, a sink, and a flea-infested bedroll. There was no stimulus, and very low illumination; as she spent her days in near darkness, they all started to blend together.

Today, however, she had a visitor.

Cass had never had a visitor, in all the many months she had been in the Dom. Or had it been years? It was impossible to know. The cell door opened, and blinding light poured in. The guard put sunglasses on her face, which helped a bit. The whole experience was still painful; even with her eyes squeezed shut the light still seemed to penetrate through the skin of her eyelids. She was led into a small, white room, so brightly lit that it hurt her eyes despite the sunglasses. A woman was inside the room, sitting in a white chair behind a white table. Her black uniform contrasted with all the white in the room, pulling her into tight focus. Cass recognized the woman's uniform; she was a Commissar, one of the Satellite Federation's political officers. Her mother had told her plenty of stories about the Commissars; this could only mean trouble.

"Miss Green, please sit down." The woman offered Cass the white chair in front of her. "How are you?"

Cassini sat. "I'm fine."

"Good. How would you feel about doing a job for me?"

"What kind of job?"

"The kind that would get your sentence commuted. Maybe you can even make some money on the side, I'd imagine someone with your skills wouldn't waste an opportunity."

"I'm listening."

The Commissar stood from her chair and paced the room, gathering her thoughts. "There are certain things that we are not, as governments, allowed to do, thanks to certain treaties, agreements, et cetera. Due to a series of...unforeseen political misadventures suffered by our government of late, there may be an opportunity to take advantage of the situation. But only if we act quickly."

Cassini peeked at the Commissar through her sunglasses. Her only thought in the moment was that her eyes were beginning finally to acclimate a bit to the ridiculously bright, painfully white room.

The Commissar realized that she was losing her audience. She'd have to try a different tack. She took a breath. "How would you like to fly to the other end of the galaxy?"

Cass was unable to process any of this. "Who are you?"

"I am Commissar Helena Nix, Cassini. And right now, I'm your fairy godmother."

8 |

TYCHO TOWERS, UNIT 2187 • COPERNICA CITY • CAMBRIA • SATELLITE FEDERATION

It wasn't the comm unit alert that awakened Max Chapman from the relative joy of deepest, dreamless sleep. It wasn't the afternoon sunlight invading through the broken blinds of his dank apartment. Or the violent rumbles of an ongoing series of distant explosions, which had apparently knocked his autographed Clive Argus image off the kitchenette wall. No, ultimately, what woke him up was a burning urge to urinate.

Wiping the saliva from his chin, he slowly, carefully made his way to the cleanroom. As he stood in front of the reclamator and began his morning routine, he looked in the mirror and saw two things: his bloated, unkempt face that was not going to win any beauty pageants today; and the INCOMING MESSAGE notification from the comm display floating inches from his face. He decided that it was probably time to start his day.

He activated the comm, and the 2-D holoscreen projected the static-laden image of...Admiral Vanakar. He silently wondered how much longer the thing would work without him paying the CosComm bill.

"Yeah," he said.

He could almost see the admiral's face beginning to fully resolve through the haze of static. "Chapman! What are you still doing there? Somehow, I just knew-"

"Always a pleasure, Admiral," Chapman interrupted mechanically, without looking up. "How may I be of assistance to you today?"

He was slowly coming out of that special kind of fog that only ten fingers of Orkney Style can manufacture. He made a mental note to order a case of Drumnadrochit next, but then remembered that with the recent Fed tax increases he could no longer afford either on his stipend. You know your quality of life is dropping when you're forced to switch to a blend like Caledonian Cask.

"Haven't you seen the news?" Vanakar asked. "No, of course you haven't." As he made his way from the cleanroom to the kitchenette, the grim glare of the admiral followed, inches from Chapman's face. "Are you even listening to me, Captain?"

He brewed some Rikichi blue tea and popped a few anti-hangover pills. "Despite the fact that I am retired, released from my commission with merits and a Green Lotus for my considerable efforts, you do indeed have my full attention."

The interference in Admiral Vanakar's transmission increased. "Chapman, there's no time, just listen to me. They're coming to get you-"

And then the Admiral's grainy image abruptly disappeared. "Your CosComm account is currently 63 standard days overdue," the helpful CosComm voice informed him, yet again. "Please contact a representative to arrange payment. Legal action will be imposed in 27 days."

"Always good to hear from you, Admiral."

Chapman took his tea over to the only chair in the place and opened the shade, letting the afternoon illumination in fully through the floor-to-ceiling windows. It was a pretty good view of the east side of downtown Copernica, from Chakram Park to the bank of the Second Severn. He received a decent pension and disability pay from his days in the Fleet, and what didn't go to rent went to case quantities of Caledonian single-malt.

After the war was over, they'd paraded him around at first. He was a hero. The Only Survivor of the Lunar Last Stand. Hero of the Prahari Line. The Only Survivor of the Sanzoku War. But the whole thing had left a lot of questions that, in their rush to celebrate, the brass hadn't thought too much about. Things Chapman himself had thought about a lot. How did he survive? Why only him? Was he really the only survivor? Or some things only the press had thought about, like: Was he somehow part of a Sanzoku plot concealing whatever insane conspiracy theory they could come up with that day? After he started showing up at events and getting pelted with expired ration bars, he quit the event circuit. After he went for groceries and got recognized and punched in the face for "killing (some guy's) pilot sister," he started staying indoors. After his childhood home on Caledon got firebombed – almost killing the family that lived there now - he moved to this high-security downtown high-rise in Cambria's capital, and kept his head down.

He saw a huge, billowing plume of dark smoke rising from one of the buildings in the distance. It looked pretty serious, but the emergency skips were already on the scene. He grabbed his macrobinoculars and peered out at the disaster. That's when he noticed the emergency skips weren't exactly doing their job; the Copernica Police and Cambrian Militia were the cause of the explosions, textbook air assault maneuvers for strategic urban demolition.

It looked like a nice enough day outside, so he wrapped himself in a blanket and brought his tea out onto the small balcony overlooking Sundaram Avenue.

"Pretty crazy, eh?"

"What?" Chapman hadn't noticed Old Man Reddy, taking some afternoon air out on the next balcony.

"The fat is in the fire now, boy. The fat is definitely in the fire," he said, aimlessly wiping the gargoyle guano from his balcony railing with an aging dishrag.

It was brighter, and colder, than it should have been. Something was wrong with the shadeshield. No doubt the old man next door knew what was going on.

"What's going on?"

"Would it kill you to join the human race once in a while?" Reddy replied. "Always locking yourself in your place like that, it's not good for you. You need to get out, hit a few of the caber bars or something, you're into all that Caledonian cack." He coughed and took a drag from his inhaler. "Governor Thakker's declared sovereignty, you idiot. All the Fed's governors have. That's the Crystal Dome on fire there."

As he was talking, a blast took out one of the spires next to the Crystal Dome, which, until a few seconds ago, was the Satellite Federation's administrative complex here on Cambria. Chapman was finally, truly, starting to wake up.

"Oh, that was a good one. These new eyes are spectacular. Did I show you my new eyes? I can see halfway across the city, I can count the freckles on-"

"But that's ridiculous. It's in the governors' interests to let the Feds handle the administrative stuff. Not to mention inter-system security, trade, representation in the League..."

"Not the way Thakker tells it. It's all about taxation and autonomy, or so she says. If you ask me, I think she just wants to run Cambria without anyone looking over her shoulder. Hey, weren't you in the Navy?"

"Yeah. Why?"

"Oh. Ho-ho!" Chapman wished the old man wasn't so giddy about all this. "Well then, I expect you'll be considered a 'Federation loyalist' then. Oh, I shouldn't be talking to you," he continued sarcastically, "I could be arrested. 'Conspiring with seditious foreign military personnel.'" Chapman heard a banging sound from inside his conapt. "That will be the Cambria Militia come to take you away, you despicable traitor." Reddy cackled. He was clearly entertained by the whole thing, but in fairness the guy was pushing 70 and therefore way past his expiration date.

Chapman suddenly realized that he was in some serious trouble. Admiral Vanakar had tried to warn him. Now what?

"Twenty-seven."

"Twenty-seven what?"

"That's how many freckles-"

There wasn't time for the old man's nonsense. The door wouldn't hold much longer; they were using a fairly high-quality battering ram. He ran back inside, past the cases of Orkney Style empties. In his wardrobe, he put on some now-snug-fitting naval trainers and g-boots. He still had his naval-issue burst pistol in the nightstand; he checked the power on the bullets and the tracker. Dead. He haphazardly stacked the cases of Orkney Style a few meters from the door, jumped behind them, and got ready. He had a lot of cases. A lot of empty bottles.

The door came down with a loud clanging crash. The room instantly filled with smoke from the doorway and the sound of thrown single malt bottles breaking on marine armor.

"Stand down, stand down!" a commanding voice...commanded. No one was firing, so Chapman clearly had them on the ropes. He peered out from behind the cases. Through the clearing smoke, he saw two carbines pointed directly at his head at very close range.

There would be no time for a daring maneuver, not that he knew any. This was it. He was about to die on his knees, execution-style. He'd tried so hard for acute self-inflicted liver cirrhosis, but in the end he just ran out of time.

"Captain Maxwell Chapman, Retired, Satellite Federation Navy?" asked a voice parked about a foot behind the carbine at his left temple, still obscured by the smoke.

"Yes?"

"Sir, I'm in command of Planetary Marine Special Forces Unit 121. We've been sent to escort you offworld. Admiral Vanakar was apparently unable to make contact with you. There's been a coup d'etat, sir, and any interplanetary military forces are being executed as traitors. Would you come with us, sir?"

"You mean you're not here to kill me?"

"Quite the opposite, sir. If you'll follow us. Please."

There was nothing to pack, and no time to pack it. Within seconds, they were in the hallway. The team kept him in the middle of their formation as they headed down the corridor. Chapman was laughably out of shape and already tired.

"Where are we going?"

"Roof, sir," replied the leader, a broad-shouldered, white-bearded sergeant who looked like he should have retired years ago. "The last transport out will pick us up. You just made it. Good thing the admiral remembered you were here. We'll take the stairs. Kendall, E.T.A. on the transport?"

A marine who was about a foot shorter than the others checked the display on her squawk box. "Two minutes," she reported.

Chapman exhaled, coughed. "You know, we could take the elevator…"

"Cute," said the Sarge. "Let's go!"

The team dashed headlong up the stairs, busting the roof access door open with a few well-placed shoulders.

There was no sign of a craft to pick them up, either on the roof or on the horizon.

"Where is it?" asked Chapman, visoring his eyes with a hand.

"Kendall?" asked Sarge, with an edge to his voice.

She checked her squawk box again, shook her head. "Lost contact, sir."

One of the other marines saw a dot on the horizon, closing fast, a gray, erratic trail of exhaust in its wake. "Sir, transport at 4:00!"

"Get in gear!" Sarge cried. "Let's go!"

The med transport - a gunship-style craft, battered, blackened and missing parts that seemed important – pulled up at the far edge of the building. They poured in the open side hatch, with Chapman still tightly in the middle of their formation. As they got themselves situated Chapman realized he was sitting next to Admiral Vanakar, who was looking a bit worse for wear; face covered in soot, laserburns on her uniform and an arm in a makeshift sling.

"Captain, due to the extreme emergency of the current situation, your commission has been reinstated."

"Yes, Admiral." What else could he say?

"Are you awake now?"

9

MEDICAL TRANSPORT VDX-11565 • OVER COPERNICA CITY • CAMBRIA

"So, what's the plan?" Chapman asked. He thought it was a reasonable question to ask, but got no response beyond the stuttering drone of the transport's overtaxed engines. His heart sank as he realized he may have traded the relative security of dying in his conapt for dying in a flying garbage can with an annoying admiral and a pack of sweaty marines. He sighed. "Is there a plan?"

"We head out to Aberle Field and take our chances," Vanakar replied.

"What do you mean, 'take our chances'?"

The platoon sergeant moved between Chapman and the admiral, blocking the captain's view of her with his significant bulk. He grabbed an overhead handle to steady himself as he looked down on the seated Chapman. "Enemy forces are on their way to Aberle, could even be there already. Maybe they're going to claim it, maybe they're going to blow it all up so no one can have it. Either way, our only ticket offworld is going to be sitting on that tarmac, but only if we get there in time." There was a long pause as Sarge stared

Chapman down. "Sir." Sarge was then distracted by something in the cockpit, and moved on to check it out.

"Enemy forces" was a bit much. Thakker and her kind were definitely bilge rats, but she and all the other satellite governors were at least duly elected. They all had run on platforms of working toward a framework of independence. If there was a mandate, there was a mandate.

Then again, mandate or not, he didn't like the idea of being physically erased as part of a state-sponsored history revision. He didn't remember anything about that in the campaign rhetoric, not that he'd paid all that much attention.

"Incoming, 1:00!" shouted the pilot from the cockpit.

"Sergeant, please save us all," said Admiral Vanakar calmly.

"Yes, ma'am," he replied. "Lopez, Snowden, suppressing fire out the side hatches."

"With these?" Lopez asked, brandishing his pulse rifle. "A little underpowered."

"Do what you can." Sarge moved to the rear of the cabin. "Fox, you're on the rear. Kendall, keep trying to raise anyone you can at Aberle. Let them know we're coming in hot but we'll take anybody with us if they want out."

"Copy that, sir," Kendall acknowledged. She was big on acknowledging.

Sarge seemed suddenly anxious, like he remembered that the grenade he gave to his nephew last year was actually live. "Captain Chapman?" he called.

Chapman looked back, twisting in his restraints in his attempt to look Sarge in the face. "Yeah?"

Sarge approached him and squatted down, addressing him quietly. "Sir, apologies for the protocol breach, it's been a long day." He stood again, his knees cracking loud enough to be heard over the engine noise. "The trick with these civil war deals is to try to get through them as quickly as possible, while also being on the side that kills the least people. The Crystal Dome had a few thousand people in it, mostly defenseless desk jockeys and low-level bureaucrats, so I'm pretty confident we've got the moral high ground for the moment."

Sarge had definitely given the situation much more thought than Chapman had. "Acknowledged, Sergeant."

There was a long, uncomfortable silence punctured finally by engine noise, taserfire, explosions, Kendall's milcomm squalking, and random shouting. Snowden was thrown from his station by enemy fire. He fell into the admiral's lap. Chapman reached under his seat for a medpack, but she touched Chapman's arm and shook her head. Snowden was dead. Chapman thought about replacing him at the port hatch, but half the port side of the transport was on fire. Sarge was already in the back, searching in vain for a fire extinguisher.

Vanakar had had just about enough. "ETA to Aberle?" she shouted forward.

"40 seconds," shouted the pilot, "if we don't get shot out of the sky first."

"We're not gonna make it," Chapman muttered to no one in particular.

The pilot shouted an expletive that Chapman had never heard before. "I've got bombers, dead ahead. They're taking out the airfield!"

Admiral Vanakar unbuckled from her restraints and headed up to the cockpit. "Bank hard left," she told the pilot, "take us off to the far side of the field, past the repair sheds."

The fire had made it to the port fuel lines, and it was short work from there to the tanks. The explosion ripped the port side wide open and obliterated both port engines. The gunship began to spiral downward.

"She's going down!" the pilot warned, helpfully.

There was a sickening noise, like various metals screaming their last, agonizing breaths, and the world turned black.

Ten seconds and a billion years later, Chapman regained consciousness. He was still strapped into his chair; the chair, however, was on its side, thrown about twenty meters from the wrecked corpse of the transport. He got started on extricating himself from the restraints. He discovered that the chair had glided along the tarmac for the latter ten of the twenty meters from the gunship, and the friction had worn away the restraints on his right side. It had also worn away half the right arm of his jacket, half the right leg of his pants, and left some nasty friction burns on those extremities. Fairly painful.

He saw Sarge emerge from the wreckage, shake his head violently as if to physically remove the cobwebs from his brain following this latest concussion, and return his helmet to its rightful place atop his grizzled head. He tapped the milcomm. "Sitrep! All units report in."

The pilot was somehow completely unscathed. He stood, leaning against the open doorway of the massive parts storage building (which he'd come only a very few meters from crashing into), marveling at his handiwork. "I got us a few hundred meters from the repair stations. Pretty close to some ships, I think," he offered to Sarge.

Sarge ignored the pilot in favor of the reports coming in from his milcomm. He went off in search of his unit.

Admiral Vanakar limped out from behind the storage shed, covered in mud and cradling a broken arm. "You're a genius, pilot," she wheezed. Chapman and the pilot ran to her, steadying her as she led them back behind the storage building. As they rounded the back corner, Chapman saw it.

"The *Pangolin*!"

"Untouched since the day we brought her back from Prahari," said Vanakar. "Repair crews were all reassigned to new construction. She's probably not in the best shape, but I think she'll still fly."

The pilot suddenly looked nervously at them. "So, um, who's gonna fly her?"

This guy had just accomplished at least twelve separate miracles of flight in the last fifteen minutes, Chapman thought, and he's worried about a *Unicorn*-class escort frigate? "You can't?"

He put his hands up. "Hey, I'm only rated for atmo. I've never even been off Cambria."

"You can't fly her, Chapman?" Vanakar asked.

"Well, if the operating system isn't damaged, once we get out in the black, I can do well enough, I can set a course heading. No maneuvers or anything. But I've never done atmo, especially not a takeoff."

"You two can figure it out." She took out her comm. "Sarge?"

"Yes, ma'am."

"How's it look?"

"Lost two more. Fredrickson and Sundstrom. I've got their tags. We're ready to move out."

"Roger that. Meet us at my position, we've got a ship."

"If we can still get inside," Chapman pointed out.

"I should still have full access," Vanakar pointed out. "I should," she repeated, somewhat more uncertainly.

They approached the nose ramp control panel. The blinking indicator on the display meant that the ship's audio interface was still functional. A good sign. "Satellite Federation Ship *Pangolin* is in repair idle mode," it said. "Please enter command code for entry."

"Vanakar 9928 Acorn."

"Thank you, Admiral." The nose ramp descended slowly, and as they boarded, they were immediately hit smack in the face with a strong rotting smell. "Would you like a tour of the ship before repairs begin?"

One of the advantages of the audio interface was the ability to walk and talk to the ship's computer. They boarded the ship before the ramp even hit the ground, and made their way to the command deck. "Negative, restore ship to active-duty mode, authorization Bluebell 147. Restore command codes for first officer Chapman, authorization...I think it was...Ibex 12?" They entered the command deck, where the rotting smell was particularly strong, and Chapman pointed out the nearby ladder to the cockpit, indicating to the pilot to begin takeoff procedures.

"Orders confirmed," the *Pangolin* replied. Chapman saw on the Operations station's status monitor the remaining marines closing the nose ramp from the inside and heading for the command deck themselves. "Tactical sensors detect incoming threats: Nine White-hall & Chaudhary SR-9 inchbombers on course to this location."

Great.

"Engage automated passive defense systems," ordered Chapman, gagging slightly. "Air exchangers on this deck at 400% for the next ten minutes." Sarge and a few of his platoon arrived on the command deck. "Sarge, are your people rated for our systems?"

There had never been a more serious person in all of space and time than Sarge at that exact moment. "Captain, we're rated for everything."

"Thank you, Sergeant," Vanakar said. She turned to the captain. "Chapman, let's get her in the air."

"Yes, ma'am."

"What are these brown stains all over the place?" asked Kendall. "I think that's why it smells so bad."

Vanakar ignored the question. "Kendall, get me Governor Thakker on the comm, would you?"

Before today, Private Kendall probably hadn't spoken to anyone higher in rank than Sarge. In the last two hours, she'd helped the Supreme Commander of the Federation fleet escape a coup, helped rescue the hero of the Battle of the Prahari Line, and now she was negotiating terms with world leaders. Chapman couldn't help thinking that it had to have been quite a day for her so far. "Yes, ma'am," she crisply replied.

Chapman had tried not to notice the brown splotches Kendall had referred to. Some were on the floor, others on walls, on console controls. Chapman suddenly realized what the brown stains were. He wasn't sure if his sudden queasiness was from his realization, or the pilot's sudden, rough takeoff.

"You guys never even cleaned the brains off the walls, did you?"

At the comm station with Kendall, Vanakar closed her eyes. She understood his anger, but this was not the time. "Like I said, Captain, it kept getting pushed down the repair schedule-"

He was surrounded by the lasting evidence of the death of his shipmates. His friends. "This ship is a tomb."

Vanakar had to get Chapman back under control. She turned to face him. "I'm sorry, Max. It's our only way out of here right now. We'll clean when we're safely out of this, I promise. For now...go help the pilot with takeoff procedures."

"What's that pilot's name?"

"Who?"

"The pilot," Chapman replied, through gritted teeth.

Admiral Vanakar stared at the captain.

"You don't even know, do you?" Chapman asked incredulously.

Vanakar took a deep breath. Chapman was probably going to get a court-martial when all this was done, but he didn't care. He didn't care about anything right now.

"Chapman, there will be time for this later. For now, get up to the cockpit. That's an order, Captain!"

Chapman slinked off to the ladder, muttering "Maybe it'll stink less up there," as he climbed to the cockpit.

Sensing that the awkward exchange was completed, Kendall cleared her throat and informed the Admiral, "I've got Governor Thakker for you."

Chapman, unnoticed by Kendall and the Admiral, climbed back down. The pilot had things well in hand, and the smell of blood and brain was, in fact, just as pervasive up there.

"Thank you, Private." The governor appeared on the comm station screen. A middle-aged woman with a permanent frown, Alina Thakker's mood hadn't improved with the success of her coup d'etat. "Governor, thank you for speaking with me."

"Admiral, I take it you're calling to turn yourself in as an enemy of the Sovereign Moon of Cambria?"

Admiral Vanakar was a soldier, not a politician. Still, she had her moments. "No, Governor. I am asking, politely, for passage through the shadeshield of your sovereign moon."

"I see no reason to allow you to escape. Surrender, and I'll make sure your execution is swift. But if you make this difficult..."

"Governor, the ship I'm transmitting from is the SFS *Pangolin*. It has a complement of one hundred experimental missile warheads, and very little to lose at this point. Two warheads would probably reduce Copernica to ash. Is that right, Sergeant?"

"Yes, ma'am, sounds about right," Sarge called out from the tactical station.

Governor Thakker paused to consider this threat. "I am in the middle of an administrative restructuring of this world's government. I do not have time for empty existential threats from a petty bureaucracy whose time is at an end." Hers was the face of someone who hadn't been expecting to be handed a loss today, but was willing to take it in stride in favor of the greater victory. "Get out of my sky." The governor terminated the communication.

"She seems fun," Chapman opined.

Vanakar spun around. "I thought I told you to get in the cockpit."

"I did," he replied, crossing his arms casually, which was incredibly painful due to the scrape on his right arm. He hoped no one noticed him flinch. "We're holding at Shadeshield Portal 47. Do we have a clearance code?"

"It's coming in now from Thakker's office," Kendall reported. "I'm relaying it to Shadeshield 47."

"Admiral," Chapman asked, "what's our heading once we get out there?"

Vanakar was tired. She plopped down at the vacant engineering station, clutching her injured arm gingerly. She thought about their plight.

"Captain, we only have one choice. The only place the Satellite Federation still exists: Laika Station."

10

SPEAKER OKWENDE'S OFFICE • LAIKA STATION • YAODONG ORBIT

Okwende was determined to stay on task, and not be taken off his game by the man who was standing – literally – hat-in-hand in his office doorway.

"Come in, Mr. Stringfellow. Please, sit down." The envoy slowly made his way to the desk.

"As usual, Mr. Speaker, I'll prefer to stand. Out of respect for the cattle, you understand." Stringfellow patted the soft leather on the back of the nearest of Okwende's chairs. "I have to leave for the Bastion in about an hour, though, so I think we might have to dispense with our usual verbal fencing and get straight to what's on your mind."

Okwende had a small object in his hand. "Fair enough. This is what is on my mind today." He lobbed the object at Stringfellow; it bounced off the Hyperion tweed of the envoy's waistcoat and landed on the carpet.

Stringfellow had made no move to catch or deflect it, but he instead leaned forward on his walking stick to peer down at it. "What is it?"

"My people tell me it's called an 'earwig.' It's a tapping device, we found it in an old pirate listening post. No clue as to the make, but I just wanted to make sure that it didn't belong to your people."

"I'm no expert, Mr. Speaker. There's no way I could determine that except to say that if someone from the Kintsugi Nation had done this they would immediately lose their rights of citizenship and be subject to whatever punishment you deem fit."

"So the team we caught trying to infiltrate the plexus mainframe on Newtonia has been, in your government's view, disavowed?"

"Mr. Speaker, there has been no organized attempt to-"

"No, Mr. Stringfellow," Okwende replied, rising from his desk with barely-restrained temper. "There have been four organized attempts. And don't worry," he added, as he saw Stringfellow's expression turn to concern, "they all managed to space themselves before we could get anything out of them."

Stringfellow shook his head, which hung low in sorrow. "I am appalled. Despite what you may think about our ways, we're not base savages. Okaasan Heika has taught us the same respect for life that the rest of the system has. These people you caught were terrorists, probably anarchists or death cultists looking to destabilize the peace. These were not our people."

It wasn't the greatest excuse, but both men knew the other was posturing. Okwende had no proof, and Stringfellow was certainly not going to admit anything. "Still," Okwende said, making his way around his desk and leaning on the front of it, "we wouldn't want the Frontier Territories getting any ideas about incursions into League space." He crossed his arms.

Stringfellow once again took the "Frontier Territories" bit in stride, not taking the easy bait. "As always, we abide by all ratified treaties and agreements. Though I have to say, those treaties don't exactly have much in the way of teeth at the moment."

"Our member nations' shipyards are working around the clock, as are yours, I'm sure," Okwende replied proudly.

"Oh, I know. Believe me, with the supercarrier Der Zweiwelten is working on, I'd sue for peace right now if I was Executive Chen." This was the first Okwende had heard about a Zweiwelten supercarrier. That class of capital ship would violate any number of treaties, as well as the League charter. Stringfellow smiled thinly. "That was a gift, Mr. Speaker, given in good faith. Please use it wisely." They stood in silence for a moment, Okwende still trying to process the whole Zweiwelten supercarrier thing. "Looks like we've run out of things to talk about for now. Listen, this has been a productive conversation, but I really do have to go."

As Stringfellow walked out of Okwende's office, he stopped at the door. "You know, something Okaasan Heika once said popped into my head not too long ago, and it turned into one of those thoughts you just can't shake."

Okwende, now eager for Stringfellow to leave so he could get in touch with his intelligence teams, replied. "And what is that?"

"Do the bars keep the mouse trapped in the cage, or safe from the cat outside?" Stringfellow smiled, placed his trilby on his head, and left.

Okwende went to his sideboard and poured a glass. He returned to his desk, silently cursing himself. He'd barely scratched the surface of topics he'd wanted to discuss.

11 |

OFS SHOJI • THE KAMBEI LINE

Captain Grafael Day sat at his command station on the cramped bridge of the *Shoji*, preparing his mind for the Mission Plea. It was his honor as captain, but he couldn't help shaking the feeling that this mission would be different, and he didn't want that feeling to intrude doubt into the Plea.

The *Shoji*, a small, *Hokkaido*-class cutter, had a complement of twelve souls, all comm and intel experts whose patience with patrol work had just about reached its limit. Finally, the *Shoji* was up for an incursion mission. Day activated the ship's comm system, took a deep breath, and represented his crew in the presence of Okaasan Heika.

"Okaasan Heika, we place our lives in your hands as we begin this mission. Let your Taisei guide us, and give us the faith to follow your orders, and the orders of your Outbound Fleet command, unquestioningly and with exceptional courage. We honor you, Heika."

"We honor you," replied the other bridge crew, and, presumably, the rest of the crew throughout the ship.

"What are our orders?" Day asked the Taisei, which was more than the ship's operating system; it was a contained extension of Okaasan Heika's own Self.

The Taisei replied in a flat female voice, "Our contact with the League's plexus network has been lost. Proceed to Belt Territory grid ID CX489G673. Investigate and restore contact. Maintain silent running while in enemy territory."

To his knowledge, no ship in the Outbound Fleet had been anywhere in the inner system in years. It wouldn't be easy sneaking in that far, but if any ship could do it, a small, quick scout like the *Shoji* could.

"All right," Day called out to his bridge crew. "You heard the Taisei. Helm, set 245 mark 3. Best speed for silent running."

"Point 65. ETA 17 hours," replied the helmsman, Shimura.

Day turned to his mission specialist. "Chuck, you got any idea where we're headed?" he asked.

Colonel Keyes was at his workstation, feverishly cross-referencing star charts with the intel report library. "Working on it now," he called back, never taking his eyes from the display. After a few more moments, he got a positive hit. "Looks like there was an abandoned pirate base on this asteroid that an enterprising ex-MOE turned into a plexus listening post."

"Sounds like a good place to sneak in and install an earwig."

"Okaasan Heika thought so too. There's been an earwig tap in this place for almost five years. Well, until a few months back, when contact was lost."

Captain Day stood up. "All right then, everyone who's mission-critical: get some rack time within the next 15 hours. I want everyone fresh for this job."

Unfortunately, everything that had been on the very small asteroid had been obliterated. The listening post was a bombed-out ruin. A freighter had been parked next to it, and all that remained of it was just a blasted – but salvageable – drive section, so whoever was responsible for all this destruction wasn't motivated by money. Day surveyed the asteroid's surface, the thin air blowing through his hair, and deduced the source of all the carnage surrounding him.

"Specials."

Keyes had his team picking apart the charred ruins of the old pirate base turned listening post, hoping to find some clues. Day walked over to him, kicked the first in a row of blackened, charred chairs in what once was a waiting room; the row disintegrated in a chain reaction. "I don't suppose we can restore our link to the plexus signal, can we?"

Keyes stood up, bringing with him a small datapad he'd picked up from from the floor. It was cracked, burned, and completely non-functional. "No. I don't think that's possible. But it looks like they left in a hurry, without doing a complete data sweep. We might get fortunate, find some useful information if we can recover enough of these." He gestured with the datapad, which promptly disintegrated in his hand. "Well, maybe not that one."

Day looked down. "Is there a basement to this place?" he asked.

"Ship scans were negative," Keyes replied. He looked around. It was a small asteroid. "Are you thinking what I'm thinking?"

Day nodded. "The Specials were clearly on a clock. We have the advantage of time, and we do have the tools on board."

Keyes called out to his team, "Fetch me the GPI."

The ground penetration imaging unit was tied into the *Shoji* team's hand scanners. Within an hour, the entire internal structure of the asteroid was mapped. And, based on the results, it was a wonder the rock hadn't broken up already.

A small maze of tunnels and void spaces, likely created by the pirates who originally settled here, left asteroid CX489G673 basically hollow inside. There were no clear indications that anyone had been down there since the early Colonial Wars, but Captain Day quoted Okaasan Heika herself as he gave the order to drill out an ingress portal: "No one knows, so let's find out."

Day donned his mission belt, and checked the charge on his rifle. "Expecting trouble?" Day asked as Keyes peered down into the darkness of the ingress.

"I don't like spiders," Keyes replied warily. "and caves are full of spiders."

"Relax," Day reassured him. "If there are any spiders, I promise I'll flick them off your shoulder or whatever."

"Thanks," Keyes sarcastically replied.

The team dropped into the tunnel system. "Chuck, take Kanno and Lange down that way," he indicated to the left.

"Aye, captain," Keyes replied, adjusting the brightness of his hand lamp. "Kanno, you'll be our navigator. Lange, keep your grip tight on that rifle. There might be spiders." He led his group into the maze, Specialist Lange briefly turning back to the rest of the team to roll her eyes at them.

"The rest with me," said Day, chuckling. As they made their way through the dusty, cobweb infested tunnel, he consulted the map on his datapad; there would be another major branch-off in a few hundred meters.

"Think we'll find any treasure down here, Captain?" asked Sullivan.

"Don't get excited, Sully," replied Norris. "Standard salvage rates apply, 50% goes straight to Gorobei."

"As it should be," Day interjected. "We're not on a treasure hunt here. We might make some prize money while we're at it, but let's focus on finding anything the Specials might have missed. Speaking of prize money, do we have room in the hold for that freighter wreck's drive system up there?"

Morita checked her datapad. "Mmm, not the whole thing, sir. Maybe just some of the key parts."

"Too bad." The tunnel ahead was sealed by a dense layer of cobwebs. "Look at this place, Chuck must be losing his mind." Day pierced the web with his rifle.

On the other side of the web, the tunnel forked off to the right. "Morita, take Sully and Shimura. And don't underreport your findings, I'll find out about it."

"But sir, you-" Shimura began to protest.

"You were just given a direct order."

"Aye, sir." They turned down the fork. Captain Day pressed forward.

According to his datapad, there were a series of smaller chambers ahead, terminating in a large void space approximately under the site of the old base. He reached the first of the smaller chambers, the light from his hand lamp revealing roughly carved, bare rock walls. No treasure crates filled with hundred-year-old pirate plunder and, thankfully for Keyes, no spiders. Still, Day was beginning to feel uneasy. The sweat on the captain's neck trickled down his back in a cool stream. He pressed forward to the next chamber.

His rational side argued that they hadn't actually seen any spiders down here. Sure, there had been some impressive webs, but they'd probably been here for the last hundred years. It was impossible to tell how long it had been since anyone had come down here; how long could spiders live without food? What could they possibly eat inside a hollowed-out asteroid? Why was Chuck's paranoia now infecting him?

Stepping into the chamber, he got answers to his questions, though he wished he hadn't.

Coveralls, spun from organic fibers, were strewn about the chamber haphazardly. A closer inspection revealed that the edges of the clothing had bites taken out of them. Also, beside and around the clothing were belts full of electrical tools; these were clearly the uniforms of installation workers, their patches emblazoned with a KleigCo logo that hadn't been used in about 75 years. Captain Day could not hold back a shiver as he observed that the clothing was filled with the clean-picked skeletons of these poor electricians who had worked down here. Been trapped down here. Died down here.

One of those clothed skeletons' arms began to move.

Day brought his rifle to bear as Chuck's worst fear was realized in front of him.

From under the skeleton a spider, roughly the size of a small cat, made its way out of the sleeve and chewed at the cuff of the thread-bare utility workers' uniform.

Day took no chances, setting his rifle from single pulse to rapid fire, and switched lamps from handheld to muzzle-end. It took all of his training, as well as infinite faith in Okaasan Heika, for him to maintain his calm and situational awareness.

The spider did not see him, or, at least, did not acknowledge Day as a threat. He told himself that this was probably the last spider left. That it had killed and eaten all the others, and was now so starved that it was resorting to eating scraps of fabric to survive.

Curiously, though, the spider did not eat the piece of fabric that its mandibles managed to remove from the skeleton. Instead, it carried the fabric away, toward the larger chamber a few meters ahead.

Grafael Day knew, somehow, instinctively, despite every fiber of his being telling him not to, that he needed to follow that spider. He pressed forward, one last time, setting his muzzle lamp to its widest beam as he entered the mouth of the final cave, following the scritching sound of the spider's shuffling legs. As he crossed the threshold, he sensed that something was truly amiss. This was also the moment when he realized that, against their protestations, he had sent both Sullivan and Shimura with Morita.

He was alone.

As he passed the muzzle lamp along the cave walls, he recoiled in disgust. His imagination would never have thought of this, certainly not the smell – a strange combination of rotting damp and sulfur.

The walls ahead and to the left were lined with what looked like melting astrocrete cylinders or spheres, the melting aspect of them obscured their true shape. They sagged from the walls. Day wondered what they were until he saw the wall on the right.

The wall on the right was lined with eggs. Pulsating, wriggling eggs, each the size of a human head. And in the far upper corner of the room, a spider the size of one of the *Shoji*'s escape pods. Hairy, with seemingly infinite legs and twice as many eyes. Barely keeping it together, he cast the muzzle lamp up to the ceiling and saw more eggs there, suspended like stalactites as far as a few meters out from the Big Spider. Beyond that, and above Day's head, more of the sagging spheres. Dead eggs, slowly rotting off the walls and ceiling around him.

He was alone.

In a cave.

Full of spiders.

He slowly activated his belt comm, and quietly announced, "Day to Team, I could...use some help over here."

"Kanno. What do you got, Captain?"

The Little Spider, having delivered the scrap of fabric to the Big Spider, finally decided to examine the invasive Outbound Fleet captain. It poked a front leg at his boot. Day let out a whispered, "Aaaaaaahhhhhhh..."

The spider then moved quickly, clamping its mandibles around his ankle. There were limits, and Grafael Day had reached his. Rather than shoot his own foot off (a thing he came very close to doing, before catching himself), he instead chose to shake the spider off with a kicking motion.

He kicked. And kicked. And kicked.

The spider's mandibles were apparently very powerful.

"Captain?"

"Just get down here. And bring a spare boot."

Day then tried to take his boot off but the spider's mandibles were simply too strong, pinching the boot tightly to his ankle. And it may have been his imagination, but it seemed like the spider was tightening his grip. The pressure on his ankle – even through the reinforced gravboot – was increasing in intensity.

He prodded at the spider with his rifle, which had the harrowing side effect of producing a rattling sound and almost imperceptible movement from the Big Spider sitting a horrifying few meters away. The other results of his prodding were equally disheartening; Little Spider's legs were solid, but its body was soft. If he shot the spider in the cephalothorax or abdomen, he'd definitely end up shooting straight through to his foot.

Good thing he told them to bring a spare boot, he thought.

He brought his rifle to bear, aiming at the spider who had now begun to secrete a trickle of some kind of acid from its mouth. Tiny plumes of smoke began to rise from the boot. His foot was all pins and needles; the pinch was restricting his blood flow.

"Day to team, how far out are you?" he asked through gritted teeth.

"Keyes here, we're close, maybe another minute. Hold tight. Ugh, these webs."

If he waited another minute, he may not have a foot. He put his finger to the trigger of his rifle, squeezing his eyes shut. He prayed to Okaasan Heika for Grace and strength.

In the tenth of a second between pulling the trigger and the rifle firing, Captain Day realized that he hadn't switched the gun back to single-shot from automatic.

Many things happened in a very short span of time.

The Little Spider was turned to jelly instantly, that jelly splattering a few feet in all directions. Thankfully, the majority of its guts did not appear to be made from whatever digestive fluid had been quickly burning through Day's boot.

The Big Spider was motivated by this turn of events to leave her perch and defend her remaining, unborn children. She unfolded her meter-long, hairy stalk legs from under herself, jumping to the floor with a jiggle from her pronounced abdomen, and she emitted a deep, hissing rattle that made the rest of the team, still a few moments and two caverns away, pause ever so briefly.

Day had put maybe half a dozen rounds into his foot, which was not as immediately painful as he would have expected – maybe it was the lack of blood flow, or the adrenaline, or the massive spider that was probably about to consume him whole. He had just enough presence of mind to bring the still-firing rifle to bear. He saw the muzzle flash reflected in the many shining black eyes of the spider as she charged him, mandibles churning and wet with burning saliva, hungry for both warm flesh and cold revenge. He screamed a war cry as she pounced, bullets penetrating through her as she knocked him to the cold cavern floor, piercing through her now-exposed underbelly as Day was given a clear shot to the spider's lower body. Day shot a spray of rounds cleanly through her cephalothorax, though the liquified results could hardly be described in the same terms.

When Captain Day finally stopped firing, what was left of the spider – the abdomen, five still-attached legs and maybe a quarter of the cephalothorax – keeled over onto the cavern floor with a squishy thud. As Day lay on the floor nearby, covered in spider guts, pieces of the cavern ceiling began to break off in small, fist sized chunks and rain down due to the rounds he had fired into the ceiling. He shielded his face with his forearm until the stone-and-egg rain had finally stopped.

Keyes and the rest of the team finally reached the cavern, though Keyes couldn't bring himself to look into the cave.

"Captain, are you all right?" Sullivan asked from the entrance.

Day removed his forearm from his face and noticed something curious buried in the ceiling, exposed by the one-sided firefight.

"Keyes, did the GPI show any hardwire conduits under the surface at all?"

This was not a topic Keyes had been prepared to discuss at that exact moment. "Uh, no," he replied, looking pointedly down at his datapad. "But the imager may not have detected them if the conduit is matched to the asteroid's local alloy content. Do you need a medic?" Shimura stepped up to the cavern mouth with a medpack.

If there was a hardwire conduit, it would have to lead from somewhere to somewhere. These spiders (what was left of them) had been living off the heat from the listening post (what was left of it) above them, so chances were good the hardwire was leading from the listening post to...

"Could it be a backup hardwire to the plexus receiver on the southern hemisphere?"

Kanno piped in. "What direction is the conduit oriented? If it was going to the receiver, it would be positioned vertically."

"No," Day replied, "I'm staring at it right now, it's running parallel with the surface. Let's get some scans, find out where this pipe goes." He propped himself up on one elbow, but it slipped on the cavern floor, still slick with liquefied spider innards. He realized that his motion was impaired for some reason, and, looking down the length of himself, noticed that his boot was covered in yellow-green slime mixed with the deep red of his own blood. "I'll take that medic now. And that boot," he said wearily, as he passed out.

Captain Day awoke in his quarters, alone.

The *Shoji* was a small ship, too small for a dedicated medbay, so Shimura and Piper had treated him here. The cabin was littered with packaging from the contents of half a dozen medpacks, as well as some specialized emergency equipment from the onboard med locker. He was attached by wires and tubes to a vital monitor. He pulled himself up to a sitting position, which wasn't incredibly comfortable in the beds outfitted by the Outbound Fleet, but after a twelve-year career he knew how to make do.

He drew back the bedsheet, revealing his swiss-cheese foot. The pain meds were doing their best, but he still felt a dull ache from his toes to his ankle. He couldn't see the extent of the damage through the bandages, but he could move his toes, so he assumed that was a good sign.

Keyes and Piper entered as Day had just begun thinking about getting out of bed. "Don't even think about getting out of bed, Captain," Piper warned. "I'll get you some more pillows to prop you up. How are you feeling?"

"Good. Fine. How soon can I get back to active duty?"

"Light duty in two days, maybe less. You'll have to wear a boot for a tenday or so. Not too bad, considering." Piper began checking the displays on the vital monitor.

Keyes was very happy to see Day alive and well. "Captain, I'm pleased to say that the mission was a success."

Day rolled his eyes. "You're just happy that your arachnophobia was vindicated."

"There is also that."

"I look forward to whiling away the next two days by reading your very detailed report on what's happened in the last – how long was I out?"

"19 hours 43 minutes," Piper interjected before Keyes could respond.

"Ugh. Anyway, just give me the short version for now."

Keyes produced a datapad. "The short version...well, you were right about that conduit. It led to a backup cache buried a few hundred meters out from the listening post. All local-alloy shielded. Captain," he looked up from the datapad, "we've uploaded the entire cache to the Taisei. Obviously, it hasn't gone wide since we're still under silent running, but locally the Taisei has been chewing on the data and we definitely got the missing few months, plus everything going back about seventeen years. It's serious stuff," he shook his head in disbelief, "we're all going to get the Star Cross for this, probably promoted even. This is the kind of data Gorobei would...what's wrong? Captain, this is-"

"Terrible news! Chuck, I'm out here to keep a low profile. I don't need a promotion, and I don't need the Star Cross on my uniform to know I know how to do my job."

"I don't get you, this is the intelligence grab of the century-"

"I guess I just don't like attention."

"Well, you're not going to get any just yet. Like I said, the Taisei has ordered us to maintain silent running. And based on its analysis of the plexus data, it's ordering us to observe some rock in the rings of Cartesia." Keyes consulted his datapad again, scrolling down a ways. "Says it's an old abandoned Special Services refitting outpost, looks like somebody's living there now and the Taisei thinks it's worth a look."

"That's good." Day seemed to brighten up at this development. "What's our ETA to Cartesia?"

Keyes put down his datapad and smiled. "You were out for quite a while," he replied. "We're already here."

12 ▌

SFS PANGOLIN · LAIKA STATION · YAODONG ORBIT

Captain Chapman oversaw docking procedures from the cockpit, his home for the duration of the journey from Cambria once the med transport pilot (a very nice man who was, it turned out, named Alasdair Cullen) got them out of atmo. The trip was largely uneventful; Chapman spent much of the time cleaning Pires' brains off the cockpit walls, screens, and viewport, and avoiding everyone else.

Since he woke up in Collinstown almost a year ago, he hadn't really processed the events that had transpired at the Prahari Line. He'd just retreated into his single-malts and tried to avoid thinking about it. But being back on the ship made it all too real for him. Cleaning the cockpit had, paradoxically, calmed him down, but he still felt like there were a lot of ghosts on the ship.

Chapman had never been to Laika Station. Not properly, anyway; he and Lex had once caught an outbound corvette from there to Prahari as part of a series of connecting rides taking them from Zavodnostadt back to the War College on Newtonia. It was her senior year (his junior), and Lex had already gotten her placement to Outpost Orange. His concentration in vexillology didn't have much use outside the diplomatic corps, but Chapman had tried to augment his course schedule with enough command courses to get posted on an active mission somewhere. Maybe even Outpost Orange, if he played his cards right.

The concept of marriage was considered extremely old-fashioned in the Satellite Federation. In the much older colonies of the inner system, the idea was impossibly archaic, like blood-letting or trickle-down economics. Strong relationships between two people, physical, emotional, even some familial connections, had completely fallen out of practice in favor of individual achievement. But Max and Lex had somehow forged a connection regardless. As they sat in the waiting area of the Federation Chancery Wing that day, faced with the thought of being away from Lex for an extended period, he'd thought that maybe the idea of marriage still had some merit. It would keep them tied together in a way, despite the vast distances that would separate them. Plus, Lex loved all that old-fashioned stuff; after all, they'd just spent a tenday at Zavodnostadt, the City of Clockwork.

Sitting in the *Pangolin*'s cockpit, where the pilot who'd served under him for nearly a year had spent his last, agonizing moments, Chapman ruminated on the way every aspect of this trip had brought back unpleasant memories. He'd already tried drowning himself in Caledonian single-malt back on Cambria, to no avail. He needed a new direction.

He noticed a spot of brain matter on the fuel gauge display, picked up the cleaning solvent, and got back to work.

The Federation citizens who had escaped on the *Pangolin* – Admiral Vanakar, Captain Chapman, a now-incomplete platoon of marines, and a lone transport pilot – looked like a motley band of worse-for-wear refugees indeed. As they disembarked, they were met at the airlock by a delegation of political heavyweights.

Chapman recognized Castor Pellas, who had represented the Federation in interplanetary politics for over 60 years. Once a paragon of vitality, he now looked ancient and pale, his eyes sunken from lack of sleep. Behind him trailed his diplomatic mission, a team of eight young men and women who looked for all the world like sailors determined to ride this sinking ship all the way to the bottom of the sea. Next to Pellas was a much shorter, much younger man in the colorful attire of his native Prahari. Chapman of course recognized him from just about everywhere; this was First Speaker Lysander Okwende, the League of Worlds' top official. Chapman tried to stay near the back of the crowd and make himself look small.

"Admiral, we're so glad you could make it," Pellas said, barely above a hoarse whisper. "Yours is the only ship to make it out of this terrible revolt."

"Thank you, Representative Pellas," Admiral Vanakar replied. "Is there any news from Kepler?" The Special Services headquarters on Kepler had been observing the governmental transition.

"Kepler has been unusually radio silent," Okwende interjected, as he led them to the Federation Chancery. "While you were en route, we forced the provisional governments to hold referendums. Our neutral observers verified the legitimacy of the results. I'm sorry to say, the Satellite Federation now exists as a political body only here on Laika Station."

"And even then, not for much longer," Pellas pointed out. "Our Charter only applies to standing governments. Once the various splinter groups are ratified, the Federation will effectively cease to exist."

"And we'll have to start work on a larger space station," noted Okwende, ruefully. "In the meantime, you may remain here until we figure everything out." Okwende stopped when they had reached the atrium in the center of the station, and addressed the group at large. "The central hub of the station is neutral territory. You may also have freedom of movement within the bounds of the Federation's Chancery Wing, but please note that no weapons are allowed in neutral areas, nor are you allowed in other Wings, unless you have compound citizenships. I have to return to League business, but I leave you in the capable hands of Representative Pellas. Thank you all for your service."

Okwende bowed to Pellas, and carried on with his day. Pellas took over addressing the crowd of refugees. "Citizens, my team will show you to your rooms. Right now, I need to speak with the Admiral privately."

Chapman's room was on the outer ring of the Federation's wing, so he had a great view of either Yaodong or Prahari, depending on the time.

Prahari, with its gleaming white spires and dense population of some of the system's most educated people, wasn't of much interest to him. He'd been there numerous times. He liked the history, the vibrant clothing styles and the erudite nature of its citizens, but he'd seen it all before. What did interest him, however, was Yaodong.

He'd of course seen images of Yaodong from before the diaspora, from what little data survived the Noble Egress era; it had looked like a blue and white jewel. Looking at it out his window now, in all its sickened, yellow-green clouded glory, he wondered how the human race could have gotten it all so desperately wrong.

All Chapman knew for sure was that, for the moment, he was safe. He took off his shoes, lay in the room's passably comfortable bed, and slept for two days straight.

He woke to see Admiral Vanakar at the foot of his bed. She was holding a garment bag, which she threw at him.

"Get up. We're going to a state dinner. Then you get to choose your new citizenship."

So much for safety.

13

THE ALAN BEAN BALLROOM •
TRANQUILITY BASE • PRAHARI

Chapman had never been a fan of state dinners. He'd had to attend a few during the War, and had thought he might see a few of the acquaintances he'd made back then, until he realized that they were probably all lost at the Prahari Line. And the realization dawned on him that, due to his unique veteran status, he was going to have to make sure that he protected that "war hero" image and watch his consumption.

They'd all arrived together, but quickly disbanded. Pellas and his diplomatic team were making the rounds with the Admiral. He noticed Sarge and a few of his marines making small talk with their counterparts from Der Zweiwelten, Prahari, and HDC. Chapman watched them idly as he nursed his Duncaster 18. It was weak, but it was apparently among the best they had on Prahari, where the locals were much more into rums and gins. He noted how comfortable the marines were while talking shop, but whenever the conversation died down, they would become immediately self-conscious - adjusting their stiff dress uniforms, straightening any medals or insignia they might have, pulling at their tight collars. Chapman agreed with them on the collar part; he'd already loosened his as much as proto-col would allow after acquiring Duncaster number two.

The League had convened this state dinner to introduce the current representatives of the governments in the Primary to the representatives from the newly-minted provisional governments of the former Satellite Federation worlds. Representative Pellas happened to be walking past, unengaged, and liquid courage compelled Chapman to ask:

"Mr. Pellas, what are we doing here?"

Pellas sized him up. "Had a few already, eh? Yeah, you kinda need 'em to make it through this. It is a long intestine, indeed."

"Lemme get this straight. You've basically been invited to your own political funeral, and you're out there bowing and smiling like you're not being cut off at the knees here, which you are."

Pellas laughed. "My boy, you do not have a head for politics, that's for sure. Look around you." Chapman looked around the room, at the diplomats and officers and ticks and leeches of industry who lubricated the works. "I have a personal relationship of some kind or another with every person in this room. I know all the major players by heart, I know what kind of gelato they're sneaking in the middle of the night.

"People like me and the Admiral, we have a wealth of knowledge and experience that would be especially valuable to any of those upstart moons smart enough to take us in. We expect our support teams to be broken up and go to the highest bidders. This is the time where we rub elbows and sell ourselves and our souls, so at the end of the day we have citizenship somewhere. Otherwise, we'll end up," he gestured dismissively, "stateless Belt pirates."

"Well," said Chapman, "that's great for all of you, but what am I supposed to do?"

"Are you kidding? You've got the best card of all of us. You're a bloody war hero."

"They burned down my house!"

Pellas waved off Chapman's concerns. "Anti-Fed sentiment. You got caught in the crossfire. Once it all dies down, you're still a winner. Any new government would just love to have 'Commodore Max Chapman, Hero of the Prahari Line' on their enlistment posters."

"Captain."

"What?"

"I'm only a Captain."

"Are you turning down a promotion, Mister?"

"Um...can you do that?" On top of that, Chapman wasn't sure the Federation Navy even had the rank of commodore.

"I'm the head of state now. Basically. Heard a few hours ago, they beheaded the Premier of Hyperion. Can you believe those silver-spooned snots? They built a guillotine. A guillotine! I'll tell you one thing; I'm not even talking to their new 'Hyperion Protectorate.' Savages." Pellas looked around the room for his next target of opportunity. His gaze focused on the bar. "You really should try some of the rum they serve here. I know it's not Caledonian whisky, but it's a whole different thing, they put umbrellas and fruit in them. Delicious." Pellas ran off to order a drink made with rum, umbrellas and fruit.

Chapman was speechless. "Well...thank you, sir." Feeling entirely out of his depth, he decided to try to find some camaraderie among the enlisted.

"Sergeant," he nodded, sidling up to the gruff, bearded marine.

"Captain," Sarge nodded in return, briefly acknowledging him before returning to his previous task, idly watching over the room.

"Commodore, actually. Just found out."

"Really? Congratulations." Sarge replied, only half paying attention. He gave a quick glance at Chapman's shoulders. "Maybe they should update your uniform. Sir."

"Yeah." Chapman searched his mind for some relevant topics to extend the small talk. "So, have you found any new opportunities here yet?"

"Yes, sir," Chapman realized that Sarge had not made any eye contact with him at all. Lex would have told him that that was not a good sign. She'd also probably have had Sarge telling amazing war stories twenty minutes ago. If she were here.

Which she was not.

He pushed forward in his conversation.

"Anything good?"

"I think so, Commodore."

"Anything you'd like to talk about?"

"I don't believe you have the clearance, sir."

"Oh. Well, good for you, Sarge."

"Yeah."

Their silence was punctured by a brief burst of laughter from a nearby group of revelers watching Pellas perform his best Clyde Stringfellow impression.

"Sir," Sarge stated, "I'm going to go stand over there now."

Chapman opened his mouth to reply, but the moment had passed; Sarge was gone.

He was alone again, still nursing Duncaster #2. There was a nearby cycad in a mahogany planter, so he decided to check it out. The leaves might be interesting.

They would certainly be more interesting than any conversation he had to offer.

As it turned out, the leaves were not very interesting. They were green, maybe two feet long, and about the width of his hand. As he bent down further to review the potting soil, a female voice behind him said, "Captain Chapman."

He spun around to see a woman, around his age, very severely dressed in black business attire and an equally severe expression on her face. She wore a Federation flag pin on her lapel, which was a nice touch. "Yes, I'm sorry, I was just...examining this...plant."

"Are you a botanist?" she asked, in a doubtful tone.

"...no."

She paused. "I see," she said, in a tone of voice which suggested that she did not at all see, but very much needed to move on.

"Also, it's not Captain anymore. It's Commodore now." He wasn't sure why he felt compelled to say this.

"Commodore?" Her eyebrows scrunched in concentrated consideration of this. "Your uniform gives your rank as captain."

Chapman laughed nervously. "I know. I was just promoted less than ten minutes ago."

"By who? Admiral Vanakar?"

"No, Castor Pellas. Apparently, he's head of state for the Federation, for however long it has left."

The woman shook her head. "While it's true that Sir Edmond Henderson-Smythe of Hyperion was executed earlier, Pellas hasn't been sworn in yet. He can't give you a promotion until he's sworn in. The Admiral can promote you, but she's been speaking privately with the Dauphin of Hong Dominion for the last twenty minutes."

"Well, that's just what-" Chapman started.

"And what would you be in charge of as a commodore? The Federation doesn't have any flight groups left to command. It's just the *Pangolin* and a few smaller ships."

"I don't think that-"

"And now that I'm thinking of it, commodore isn't even a current Federation rank. Only Der Zweiwelten Cosmoflot uses it, for their high command flag officer."

Who was this woman? "Who are you?" he asked.

"I've got to say, I'm not impressed." She grabbed a glass of champagne from a passing waiter. "Don't tell people you've been promoted until they give you the shoulder boards to prove it. And tighten that collar."

And she walked away.

"Still making friends, I see," said a voice to his right. A voice that was somehow familiar and unfamiliar at the same time. Chapman turned to see a completely bald man he didn't recognize who, again, clearly had the advantage. "Aw, I'm not going to let you sweat. Rand Talmadge. We were podmates on Hibernia. Fifth levels? Miss Shaikh, Pod 207?"

Chapman was happy to see a familiar face, even if it was one he barely remembered from his childhood. "I remember! Randy Talmadge, best climber in the pod."

"Still am, really," Talmadge laughed. "But now I do most of my climbing politically."

"Yes, well then, what brings you here to this..." what had Pellas called it? "...intestine?"

Talmadge looked at his gin & atmo and considered this question. "I don't know if you're going to believe this," he said, "but I'm now the Primary representative for the Greater Kernow & Hibernia Confederacy."

"Doesn't exactly roll off the tongue, does it?"

"It's been a race against time to secure the good names before they're taken by the others. It's pretty cutthroat out there - I mean literally. It's mostly been isolated incidents, but some people are actually getting violent over some very petty stuff right now. I've never seen anything like it. We're trying to police it as much as possible, but we're all limited in what we can do."

"Sounds like you've got a lot on your plate."

"It's true. I could definitely use some help. You know, since you were born on Hibernia, I can get your citizenship fast tracked if you were interested in helping us out."

"Well, uh, what do you need?"

"What we need to do is get all these different governments together, agree to some basic neighborly codes of conduct, standards, borders, all that. A lot of this stuff is already in place from the Fed, but we need everyone to agree on them again, ratified. And really, to most people it sounds so minor but I know you of all people understand the importance of flags."

"Oh, absolutely."

"I remembered how in History, you would always sketch these wonderful flags in your datapad. And then of course after the War I find out that your War College concentration was in vexillology, at which point I said to myself 'I have got to reconnect with this guy.' If nothing else we'd love for you to run our Commission on Visual Representation." He paused. "It's bad, Max. It's really bad."

"Well, I don't know if-"

"Max. They want our flag to be the confed seal centered on a black background with 'HIBERNIA' in white block letters above it, and 'KERNOW' below it."

"Holy trots," Chapman replied, mortified. This was a true vexillogical emergency, if there ever was one.

"I don't need an answer now, but we'd love to have you back on Hibernia, and we'd love it if you came to work for us. We'll make the money right for you, whatever you need."

It was a tempting offer. "Wow," Chapman said, "that really is a tempting offer. Can I think about it?"

"Hibernia's not going anywhere, my friend." Talmadge slapped Chapman on the back. "Take all the time you need. Things probably won't get really full-scale violent for another tenday or so."

Chapman laughed at what he hoped was a joke. "Ok, I'll try to get back to you sooner than that. And Rand, thanks for thinking of me."

Talmadge started backing up slowly, drifting his way into a crowd of Praharan dignitaries. "You bet! It's definitely been good to see you, Max. Contact me!" Talmadge called back to Chapman from somewhere deep in the crowd, as he let the wave of people wash him away.

And then he was alone, again.

"Excuse me, are you Captain Maxwell Chapman?" said a voice behind him. He wished that, just once, someone could walk up to him in the direction he was facing. He turned and almost walked into an ancient Greek statue, life-like painted.

Except the statue was an actual living woman, and was the one who had addressed him. "Captain?" she asked again, in more of an introduction now, offering a dainty hand to him palm-down in Zweiwelten fashion.

Chapman accepted her fingertips and bowed slightly, in what he hoped was the correct response. This was definitely Someone Important; if he could manage to keep it together who knows where this could lead. "I am Captain Chapman. Honored to meet you, Madam."

"You...don't know who I am?"

He looked down at his whisky glass awkwardly. "I'm afraid you have the advantage. This," he gestured, indicating the room full of Important People, "this isn't really my territory."

"And what is your territory, Captain?"

He laughed, and thought for a moment. "A tall ship, and a star to steer her by?"

"Spoken like a true romantic, Captain. Not many of you left, these days. Have you spent any time in the Floating World?"

"I once spent a tenday of leave at Zavodnostadt. That was the only time, I'm afraid."

"The City of Clockwork is not what it once was, I'm sorry to say." She stared off to the side, either in thought or momentary distraction, Chapman wasn't sure which. The woman was young, but in that moment she seemed decades older. "Nothing is what it once was. If it ever truly was, to begin with." She broke from her reverie. "At any rate, my name is Darinka Korovenko, Duchess of Ravenscar. You may address me as Duchess."

"I am again honored, Duchess."

"I'm also Der Zweiwelten's representative to the Primary, and I'd like to give you a tour of Tranquility Base if you have a moment."

"Right now?"

"No time like the present."

He took one last look around at the room full of Important People, and downed what little remained of his Duncaster. "Let's do this."

They had walked through the Hall of Astronauts, the Hall of Cosmonauts (the Duchess stopped here and spent a few minutes pointing out a few of her own personal heroes), and Tereshkova Hall, the first meeting place of the old Solar Nations, from back before the Colonial Wars. Now, as they traversed a long hallway filled with statues of the early statesmen of the SN, they approached a large, antique geodesic dome. At the doorway was a bronze plaque.

STATIO TRANQUILLITATIS

They entered the dome. Inside was a sparse network of walkways over bare lunar soil, and a large metal construct. As they got closer, he remembered the metal thing from Remedial Spaceflight. It was the landing module from the Eagle.

"It's been a while," Chapman said. "I don't think I've been here since our trip in 2nd Level pod."

He read some of the museum-style displays about the astronauts and the Apollo 11 mission. He watched a brief, grainy old 2D video of the astronauts. One piece showed an aged astronaut punching people in the face for saying he hadn't been to the moon, and shouting epithets at the moon from pre-Egress Yaodong with a younger woman whose contextual presence was unclear. At another nearby display, the Duchess read aloud from the plaque those intrepid explorers left behind:

"Here, men from the planet Earth, first set foot upon the moon. July 1969 A.D."

Chapman remembered the rest. "We came in peace for all mankind."

"Signed, Richard M. Nixon." As she stepped, her gossamer dress somehow never moved, making it look as if she was floating toward him. "Captain, I was wondering if you might be willing to volunteer for a...a project that some of us have been working on."

There it is. "What did you have in mind?"

"About twenty years ago, a project was started called Operation Second Egress. The League states had gotten together and decided to start exploring outside the solar system, get a head start on future colonization efforts, that sort of thing."

"I know a little bit about this. At the War College, one of our instructors was Dr. Kerensky. He'd headed up something called Project Iditarod. Something about extra-long-range satellites. He wasn't allowed to say much about it, except that it had been suspended because of the Treaty of Kambei."

The Duchess smiled. "It had been suspended, but not before the Iditarod probes were launched. A fact that the Frontier never found out about. We've got scores of deep space probes mapping out our stellar neighborhood right now. There's been a team working on the data, in secret, for the past twelve years. They've also been working on some other things. Ultra-lightspeed travel, for instance."

"Don't tell me they've got a working FTL drive."

"The problem hasn't been getting things to go at lightspeed - the Iditarod probes are actually screaming through space right now at plus 3c – the problem, and they've almost worked it out, is getting *living* things to go past lightspeed without dying horribly, instantaneously."

Chapman suddenly got the feeling he was about to be asked to die horribly, instantaneously. "Where do I fit into all this?"

"Destiny herself has shined upon you, Captain." The hard sell. Chapman's internal alarms were blaring. He didn't believe in destiny, upper- or lowercase D, despite what he'd been through. "You're the soon-to-be stateless captain of a soon-to-be stateless spacecraft. The Treaty won't apply to you if you cross the Kambei Line in the brief time before your moons' independence is ratified. And, with a little refitting, the *Pangolin* is the perfect ship to take out an expedition to find new worlds to settle."

"Frankly, Duchess, no disrespect, but I'm not sure I want to die horribly, instantaneously or otherwise."

"I understand. The research teams have the *Pangolin*'s specs and are preparing tests as we speak. I wouldn't be here if they weren't confident."

"And if I say no?"

"We can get someone else," she conceded. "But the legal standing will be weaker. The Frontier's spynet is...formidable. There's no way we can fully prevent them from knowing we've sent you out there, especially since you'll need to pass through their territory to leave the system. So, we'd really need a ship and command crew who will have no legal ties to the treaty. Otherwise, we'll all be in violation, and we don't need another war, especially not now."

He looked at the 2D video again. It was on a loop, so it had repeated several times during their conversation. "I walked on your face!" the astronaut, the irrepressible Aldrin, yelled, shaking a still-potent fist at the distant moon. Chapman looked down at the lunar soil, with the permanent footprints of these men, now dead for centuries. He understood now why she had brought him here, with her talk of Destiny and history, appealing to his sense of duty.

But he saw it differently. Off a few yards away, he saw the American flag the astronauts had planted standing, inert and lifeless, near the lunar module. He thought of the flags of Hibernia and the other Federation worlds, and how he would spend hours staring out the window of the learning pod, ignoring his studies, just watching the flags wave in the wind. They moved freely, independently, motivated by an invisible force; a living symbol of government as an ideal.

Maxwell Chapman had exactly zero interest in politics, but he understood a few things about symbolism, motivation, hope. Conditions in the system proper were on the edge of something dangerous, and the Duchess was looking for something positive to point to, a place to start over – if she could find one. She was looking for that grand old image of a new flag waving in the sunset sky of a new home.

Yaodong was already a toxic wasteland; the rest of the solar system would be the next to burn. It was time to move on. And maybe, if possible, leave all the self-destruction behind.

It was the kind of job Lex would have taken, in a heartbeat.

He sighed. He was ready for Duncasters 3 through 6. "What the hell," he said. "You've gotta die of something."

14

SOUTHEAST FIELDS · BLUE SECTION · KONFURAWABURU FARM · SLATEFIELD · HEIHACHI · TENNOSEI · THE KINTSUGI NATION

Major Vivian Sato downshifted her Arctor Nine Treadaway as it climbed the mud-soaked incline to the intersection of the Blue and Orange service roads. The wipers cleared the persistent rain from her field of vision as she tried to figure out whether to turn right or left onto the Orange service road. Today's storm had been wreaking havoc with the Nine's autodirectional systems, and, frankly, she had more important things to do than get lost in the middle of her own farm.

It was her husband's farm, really; millet and springwheat had been grown here by Matt's family for three generations. Matt wasn't much of a farmer, but he was an only child, so eventually the farm had been left to him. The farm basically ran itself as long as they hired enough hands, so while Matt and Vivian Sato pursued careers in the service of Okaasan Heika, the farm chugged along as it always had. They told themselves one day they'd retire here and take a more active role.

Then Matt developed the Roga. Six months later, he was gone. It happened so fast, the Major barely had time to make it out to say goodbye at the treatment center on Satsuma.

Out in the Frontier, where things are always a bit different from the rest of the system, it was almost unheard of for anyone to contract the Roga. It had been an inner system plague for decades, only spreading as far out as the Federation. No one at the treatment center could understand how a farmer from Heihachi who'd never left the moons of Tennosei could have contracted the Roga.

The Major knew exactly how it happened. But if she told them, she'd have to kill them.

Matt and Vivian Sato had worked for the Shujutsu, a branch of the Outbound Fleet tasked with a variety of...clandestine operations in the service of Okaasan Heika. While the kids thought their parents were on Katsushiro trying to secure renewals of their springwheat contracts, Matt was drilling microscopic holes into the shield emitters of Nizkistadt, while Vivian quietly ruined the career of a prominent Prahari politician. When Matt died the way he did, it effectively blew their cover. Vivian came clean to her children as much as she could: thinking on her feet, she spun a quick yarn about her and Matt doing some agrisupply consulting for the Outbound Fleet, her rank of Major bestowed upon her honorarily. In reality, she'd earned every inch of her stripes in brave, cunning service to Okaasan Heika.

The member nations of the League of Worlds deserved much worse than the low-key destabilization the Shujutsu practiced, in the Major's opinion. But, if history had taught her anything, she knew those decadent governments would die of bloat or rot from within more than anything, and the Kintsugi Nation would be ready to take advantage of any weakness.

The cost, though - for her at least - was almost unbearably high.

She slammed the Nine into a higher gear, and turned right down the Orange road.

The exchange module for the millet field's wastewater pump was easily fixed. If she hadn't gone out here herself to prove a point to the farm's foreman, it would have been fixed earlier this morning by one of the help. "Ted," she told him, "sometimes you have to lead from the front." She didn't ask anything of her people that she wasn't willing to do herself. Somehow, that attitude never extended to their children, who never joined the family business. Either family business.

Their daughters, Cassia and Lanai, both married into good families (the Major had made sure of this). Cassia was a high-level administrator for the state utility service, and Lanai was a very successful mural artist for the Public Relations Service.

Their son, Bruce, was a toymaker. He left home at 18 and hopped a smuggler's ship to Cerigo. The Shujutsu had operatives who took care of people like Bruce in a permanent sort of way, but no one was willing to take out the Major's son, so there he stayed. The Major found herself, out in the millet field, sitting on a metal wastewater pipe in the driving rain, thinking about her son for the first time in a while. Was he still making little clockwork people in some Eurotourist trashtown in Der Zweiwelten? Would he ever be ready to come home?

Even if he was ready to come home, he'd never help with the farm. None of the children had any interest in it whatsoever, mostly because farm business was what they'd long perceived took their parents away from home so much. Those kids would never truly know the sacrifices that the Sato family had made in service of Okaasan Heika.

Thankfully, those days of sacrifice were at an end.

The Major reached back and squeezed the rainwater from her coarse, soaked white hair. She'd been semi-retired now for almost six months, if one could call managing a millet farm on Heihachi and skipping out to oversee regular training exercises "retired," but without Matt, it gave her very little joy. The brightest spots in her day were her grandchildren, Opal and Gedde. Like most grandparents, she was probably subconsciously using them to make amends for her mistakes as a parent, but if anyone had a problem with it they could take it up with her.

Which reminded her, she had a very important appointment in only three hours' time.

15

CAREER DAY • MISS McKEE'S THIRD GRADE CLASS • PINE CITY PRIMARY SCHOOL • HEIHACHI PREFECTURE • TENNOSEI • THE KINTSUGI NATION

"Thank you so much, Mrs. Takara, for showing us how important hydroponic farming is to our community. Let's give her and Mitsuko a big hand." Ms. McKee, a middle-aged woman in a blue gingham dress, led the class in a round of polite applause. "Now, Opal Harriman is going to introduce her grandmother, and tell us about what Mrs. Sato does."

Opal, the younger of the Major's two grandchildren, got up from her desk and trundled to the front of the classroom. She has absolutely no performance anxiety at all, the Major marveled as she waited in the wings at the side of the room with the other parents and grandparents, which was more than the Major could say even for herself.

"My grandma's name is Vivian Sato. I think she's the best grandma ever because when she goes away for work I know she misses me because she always brings me home something from wherever she went, to teach me about the places she sees."

"Opal, tell us what your grandmother does," Ms. McKee prodded.

"She's a Major in the Outbound Fleet." Sato's work for the Shujutsu obviously wasn't the kind of thing you told your grandkids.

"And what does the Outbound Fleet do, Opal?"

Opal beamed. "They protect Okaasan Heika and all her Children from the bad people!"

"Thank you so much, Opal. Now, let's bring your grandmother up and we can ask her some questions."

"Yay!" the children cheered, finally getting to the action after all the sleepy stories from the mundane citizens who were farmers and cobblers and ditchdiggers. The Major herself had almost fallen asleep during the minor-professional cricketer's explanation of how the game worked, though a few of the sportier kids were interested.

As she made her way to the front of the classroom, Major Sato made quite an impression on the kids in her rather ridiculous dress uniform. But, according to the Public Relations Service, that was the point, and why she was compelled to attend as many of her grandchildren's functions as her "retirement" assignments would allow. She'd have done it gladly anyway, just not with all the resplendent majesty of the absurd dress uniform.

As she looked out over the twenty or so children in the class, she was more nervous than she would have been if she were briefing the Pontifex himself. Still, she had enough of a command presence that she knew how not to show it. She cleared her throat. "Major Sato, KOF. I think Opal pretty well covered the basics, but I'll take a few questions." From the sea of raised hands, she made eye contact with a girl a few rows back. "You."

"I was wondering where are all the places you've gone."

Major Sato smiled. "Well, I can't tell you all the places I've been," she replied, to which the whole room chuckled, "but I can say that I've been to all the moons of Kennosei and Tennosei, and all the moons of Meiousei except for Tokyoto." Another hand, this time a girl near the corner. "Yes?"

"Is it true that children in the inner system don't have families?"

Sato considered the question carefully. She wasn't sure how far she could go on this topic with a bunch of third-graders. "Not entirely. In the inner system, when a person wants to start a family, they go to a consulting clinic. Their genetic material is extracted, they discuss the kind of child they want to raise, and nine months later they are given a baby. The worlds have different limits on family sizes; I think the most is Prahari, with four."

"Except for Hong contracts, they're all slaves," said a precocious boy sitting near the teacher's desk. Sato could tell immediately that he was trouble.

"Hong Dominion has free citizens as well, but by some definitions I suppose you could say that contracts are slaves. Contracts have no reproductive rights or abilities, so within the Dominion contracts don't have families as we know them here, but there is a familial relationship within groups of them raised together, similar to brothers and sisters. No parents. You'll like that idea in a few years." While the idea was horrifying to the children, who were indoctrinated from very early on to love and respect their parents, some parents in the room remembered their rebellious teen years and chuckled. Another hand, this time a stout young man about halfway back. "You."

"How do I join the Outbound Fleet?"

"Did the PRS plant you in this class?" Sato joked. Cue polite laughter.

"No," replied the boy, matter of factly.

Yes, they would love this boy in the Fleet. No sense of...anything. "Right, well, if you keep your studies up, and put in an application to Satsuma or Rikichi, you might get accepted. The most important thing we look at is your grades, though, so make sure you do your best in your studies!" From a moral standpoint, it wasn't easy to lie this boldly to a room full of kids, especially when mandatory Academy pre-enlistment at fifteen had been the regulation for the last fifty years. All education was a path to some form of service to Okaasan Heika; their only choice was their method of service. But the parents appreciated having an authority figure telling the children to work hard; when they said it at home for the millionth time, they could add, "Remember what Major Sato said!"

A young boy in the front row, who had until now been staring at his desk, blurted out, "Is the war really over?"

"Please raise your hand, Bernard," Miss McKee chided.

"It's all right," Sato said, trying to add as much kindness as possible to her voice, as Opal had told her about her new classmate Bernard. She knelt down to get closer to eye level with the boy, whose eyes were welling up with tears. "Bernard, did you lose family on Shin Honshu?"

Bernard nodded. "I came here to Heihachi to stay with my grandparents for the summer last year," he said, pausing to sniffle, "and the Sanzoku came and I've been here ever since. I miss my friends, and..."

"And your mother and father," Sato finished. "We all lost people in the war. But maybe none so profoundly as you, Bernard." She stood up, patted poor Bernard on the head comfortingly. "But, to answer his question, the answer is yes. The Sanzoku War is over.

They are never coming back; I can tell that to you for a fact. Okaasan Heika has told us so. However," and this is the part she had to practice in the mirror when no one else was around, "we don't know what else is out there. And we're out here on the frontier of the solar system. We are the first line of defense. So, we have to be ever vigilant, to make sure nothing like the Sanzoku War ever happens again. Heika be praised."

The predictable patriotic applause followed, as it always did.

This was the easy part of the job.

An hour later, it was all over.

The children had gotten their hugs and gone back to their lessons, and their relatives all milled around the school's lobby, waiting to be officially dismissed. The major was engaged in what may have been the most boring conversation of her life (which was truly saying something), a very one-sided discussion of mulch types with a woman whose hair looked as if it were this close to sliding off her head entirely, to make a go of it in a new and very distant land.

"...and really, the cultured birch has a great scent, and is engineered to repel bilge rats and cockroaches-"

A squat, toadlike man approached the major and Madam Birchwood. "Excuse me. Major Sato?" The amount of sweat coming off his brow was impressive.

"Yes, I'm Major Sato."

"Headmaster Watanabe, ma'am. If you'll come this way, there's an urgent communication for you."

"A communication?"

"Yes, ma'am. From the Bastion, ma'am."

"The Bastion?" She turned to her new, mulchy friend, her eyes wide for dramatic effect. "The Bastion. Please excuse me."

Headmaster Watanabe led the Major down a labyrinth of hallways to the school's faculty comm room. "I don't think we're set up for a communication from the Bastion, ma'am," Watanabe fretted apologetically. "It's only a commercial system."

"It's fine," she replied. "I have a variety of encrypted frequencies I can use." They reached the door to the comm room. "Is there any other entrance or exit to this room?"

"No, ma'am."

"Windows? Ventilation?"

"No windows, there are some vents but they're particle filtered."

"Good. Guard this door until I say otherwise, Headmaster. No one gets in until I come out. Do you understand?"

"Absolutely, ma'am."

"May Okaasan Heika protect you."

"And all her Children," he replied, bowing deeply.

She entered the comm room, locking the door behind her.

The room was outfitted with a Sternkeel 80 comm transceiver; full 3D holo in monochrome. It was what you'd expect from a decently funded school, but not exactly ideal resolution quality for speaking with the Bastion. Despite the headmaster's claims about security, she noted the room's ceiling was drop-tiled. She determined at that moment to make her exit from the school via this ceiling, apparently vanishing without a trace and effectively leaving the headmaster guarding the door for the rest of his life. This would also serve to reinforce the air of mystery surrounding her in the local community. Time was of the essence, though, so she got down to business and entered her most secure personal frequency code. After a moment, the room lights went down and the image of the Pontifex himself resolved from millions of tiny lines of light.

"Your Grace, I am honored," she proclaimed, bowing her head and going down to one knee with palms outstretched in the typical protocol.

"It is I who is honored. Your many decades of service have been noted by Okaasan Heika herself. Your work in the Kerensky affair is still discussed in strategy circles to this day."

"I am but a humble servant of Okaasan Heika."

"As are we all," he replied. "Please rise, that we may speak as equals in service." She rose. "Time is short, so I will endeavor to be brief. I bring news of a captain in the Outbound Fleet named Grafael Day."

"I am unfamiliar with him, your Grace."

"It's not surprising; the man has a knack for avoiding attention. Captain Day's ship, the *Shoji*, failed to return for his ship's scheduled crew turnover. Last known coordinates had it crossing the Kambei Line to restore our tap on the MOE plexus. It was the fourth ship we'd sent out there since the tap was cut off; the first three were lost. The *Shoji* was ordered to remain under silent running until its mission was completed, and that seems to have happened - we do have the tap restored. But they haven't checked in yet, which means they've either been destroyed on their way back..."

"Or the mission parameters have changed," Major Sato finished.

"Either way, there's no way to know their current status. We have a lot of irons in a lot of fires right now, Major. A ship out of communication on the other side of the border is...an unwelcome variable in Okaasan Heika's calculations."

"Do you believe he's gone rogue?"

"There are many possibilities, we simply don't know. As I said, merely a variable. But one which must be dealt with all the same. Okaasan Heika has determined in her infinite wisdom that you should be tasked with resolving the situation."

"What is Her desired result?"

A soothing female voice intoned, "There is biology. There is vengeance. And then there is justice."

The Pontifex seemed as taken aback by the voice as the Major was. "You, ah...appear to have your answer, Major, such as it is. A shuttle will arrive for you tomorrow to take you to the *Dauntless*. Captain Sakamoto will then brief you on any details. Good hunting."

The image of the Pontifex disappeared. The room lights came up.

Major Vivian Sato was no longer retired.

16

SFS PANGOLIN · EN ROUTE TO KESTREL BASE

Chapman was confined to the quarter deck for the trip out to Kestrel Base, as were a few personnel he recognized from Sarge's marine platoon, and some other people he didn't recognize. One person he glimpsed while boarding that he did recognize was that incredibly rude woman from the reception on Prahari. He hoped she was some kind of bureaucratic staff and wouldn't be assigned to the mission.

Admiral Vanakar was given command of Operation Second Egress just before leaving Laika Station. It was the final act of Castor Pellas' very brief term as head of state. A few hours later, Pellas stepped down and was hired as an advisor to the board of the Runciter Corporation, and the *Pangolin* was off to some mysterious top-secret installation that was so classified everyone but a random pilot was sequestered on one deck for the duration of the trip.

Pellas never did give him that official bump up to Commodore, either.

It would take a day to get wherever it was that they were going, so he figured he'd have to do something to keep busy. Looking around the cabin, he decided to clean things up a bit, since the place was a total mess.

They'd given him his old cabin from his last tour. Ironically, he had more personal effects here than he'd lost in his firebombed house on Caledon, or left behind on Cambria. In a sense, he was truly home.

As he picked up the books that had been thrown from the bookshelf during one crazy maneuver or another at the Prahari Line, there was a chime at the door.

"Yeah," he acknowledged.

The door opened. It was, of course, the rude woman from the reception. Instead of the severe business suit, she was wearing a severe Commissar's uniform. Great, just what this team needs: a political officer.

"Captain, do you have a moment?"

"I have one standard day."

She stepped inside, looking around, carrying something brown and lumpy in her arm. "Making yourself at home already, I see."

He replaced the antique books on the bookshelf above his desk. "I had a two-year head start on the rest of you. What can I do for you, Miss...?"

"I'm sorry," she said in a tone that explained that she was only sorry that she had been caught in a social faux pas. She bowed slightly. "Commissar Helena Nix, Federation Office of Political Affairs."

Chapman bowed his head slightly in return. "Good to meet you, Commissar." He then turned his attention to making his bed.

"As you had requested your earlier assigned quarters, it seems I've been placed in Captain Houlihan's former cabin." This got Chapman's attention. "I thought, as Captain, you might want it." She extended the lumpy brown thing at him; as he reached out for it, he recognized it as Houlihan's old bomber jacket.

"He'd just gotten a new one before we were deployed to the Prahari Line," he said, running his hand over the various mission patches adhered to the jacket's arms. "Much obliged, Miss Nix." He hung the jacket on a coat hook near the door.

"I'm very glad to see you making yourself comfortable, Captain," Nix said. "I...have had my concerns about you in relation to this mission, and I feel it's only fair to tell you up front that I fought very hard to keep you off the roster."

"Thanks for your honesty," Chapman replied, returning to tucking his blankets under his pillow.

"My concern is that you were, or are, suffering from a malaise which may have an adverse effect on your judgment in a command capacity. Also, you suffer from a clear chemical dependency, namely, Caledonian whisky. You may also have unresolved stress trauma."

"Commissar, do you see any Caledonian whisky in this cabin? I'll save you the investigation: you don't. There isn't any. When I was an XO, I didn't drink on board the *Pangolin*. Command is a three-shift job; there's no time to be impaired. When we get to Kestrel Base, during the refit, I might have a drink or two when I'm off duty. But aboard this ship, on active duty as the captain? Negative, ma'am."

Nix was unprepared for the lecture. "Well. That's good, then. I will be depending upon you a great deal in the coming tendays as we get this expedition prepared, and I will need a ship's captain who is focused and able to obey my orders without hesitation."

"Now wait just a second," Chapman objected, "I'm in command of the ship. A political officer is outside the command structure, you observe and report. And stay out of my way."

"That is usually true," Nix replied, "but as it pertains to Operation Second Egress, I've been given authority over the mission. As captain, you will of course have full authority over the ship and crew. However, all aspects of the mission itself are under my purview, and that includes situations where ship's crew are directly supporting the mission."

He realized that she was right. That kind of arrangement was within protocol in extraordinary circumstances. "Understood." He suddenly felt like taking a nap. "Well, I look forward to working together with you on this mission." He stood and bowed to her, a deep and exaggerated courtly bow that he hoped signaled to her that she shouldn't expect him to take her 100% seriously.

Nix returned his bow with a curtsy that was equally ridiculous under the circumstances, and also monumentally awkward coming from her. "Thank you, Captain." Maybe she had a sense of humor in there somewhere after all, he thought as she left his cabin.

He took a pull of Drumnadrochit from his boot flask. He was serious about what he'd said to Nix, but he wasn't in command of anything for another eighteen hours, either.

They had given him a datapad with extensive notes on the upcoming operation. If Nix was going to be riding him like he thought she would, he'd better start studying.

17

OFS DAUNTLESS · TENNOSEI ORBIT

The Major's shuttle landed in the *Dauntless'* main shuttlebay. As she exited the shuttle, she was greeted by Captain Sakamoto and his adjutant. They all exchanged bows as she approached them. The Major elected to remain in motion, causing the captain and his adjutant to rush to catch up as she made her way out to the corridor.

"Have you received your orders, Captain?"

"Indeed we have, Major. We're to maintain silent running-"

She stopped short, and turned to face the captain. "All orders regarding this mission are not to be discussed outside of Level 3 security areas. Is that clear?"

"Very clear, ma'am." They continued down the corridor. Sakamoto led them to the lift that would take them to the bridge, and waited until they were aboard with the doors closed to resume any conversation. "I trust your shuttle trip was uneventful."

"It was, Captain."

The lift hummed quietly.

"It seems this season's Caspian flu casualty numbers are much lower than projections."

"That's good news, Captain. The citizens of Kyuzo have had their faith in Okaasan Heika rewarded once again."

The lift continued to hum quietly.

"Is it still raining on Heihachi, Major?"

"Are you writing a book, or are you just willfully obtuse, Captain?"

"Apologies, ma'am."

The lift door opened, mercifully relieving the tension that had been building like static electricity within. "Lead on, Captain. We can dispense with formalities; I don't need to be introduced to your crew. I'll discuss our orders with you personally, in your wardroom, perhaps. Immediately, please."

They exited the lift onto the bridge. "Captain on the bridge," announced the adjutant. They marched to the wardroom, on the opposite side of the bridge. The adjutant peeled off as soon as possible to look on with the tactical officer as she examined a particularly uninteresting display.

As the wardroom door closed behind them, Captain Sakamoto felt a cold sweat begin to form in the small of his back. He sat at his desk, more to get the Major out from behind him than anything else. "Have a seat, Major," he offered.

"I'll stand, thank you." Of course. "Taisei," she called, addressing the *Dauntless* computer, "run protocol Rosewater Elgin." She smiled. "Just a bit of privacy. There are some things that future generations may not understand, so why confuse them with a record?"

"Indeed, ma'am."

"Captain, we are going to find a potentially rogue cruiser that's crossed the border into League territory. We're either going to bring it back, blow it up, or maybe a third option, I'm not yet sure. But probably blow it up."

"The *Dauntless* will serve Okaasan Heika in any way possible. It is our honor to serve."

"That's the most intelligent thing you've said all day, Captain."

18

CREW QUARTERS QP3 • SFS PANGOLIN • KESTREL BASE • LOCATION: UNDISCLOSED

Cassini awoke with a start when the *Pangolin* landed. It was the first time in recent memory that she'd been a passenger on a ship instead of a pilot, and she couldn't say she was all that comfortable with the experience. She had no idea where they'd landed, but if she had to guess she'd intuit that they were orbiting Cartesia based on the feel of the gravity. She freshened up, grabbed her duffel, and headed out.

The ship's corridor was crowded with people, all on their way somewhere. Cass let herself be carried by the current of people heading off the ship. Some looked official; military types, or ex-military – they all had that indoctrinated, lock-step bearing she knew all too well. She could easily identify the civilians; techs, grease monkeys, some normals probably there as consultants. Those heading into the ship were all techs, looking eager to tear the ship apart and remake it into whatever form the mysterious powers that be had dictated.

More than anything else, Cass was ready for some answers.

At an intersection, her crowd merged with another exit-bound crowd, this one led by Commissar Nix with a man wearing a stegskin jacket that looked suspiciously similar to Cassini's own. The pair appeared to be in a heated debate.

"Are they going to be confined to quarters for the whole journey?" he asked. "Because maybe they should be."

"Once we get out there, they'll all fall in line. Don't underestimate the human ability to cooperate under life-threatening conditions."

"As long as they don't threaten my life in the process. The unnecessary risks – what the cack?" The man in the jacket stopped short so as not to trample on a foot-tall Fellswoop drake.

"BRAAAAAAK!" exclaimed the Fellswoop, flapping its wings and puffing its chest in challenge to the man.

"Why is there a gargoyle on my ship?" he asked.

"Your ship?" the Commissar asked.

A young woman fought through the oncoming crowd to grab the budget-sized dragon. "Sorry! Sorry. He got away from me."

"We're letting pets on this trip now?" the man asked Nix.

"I had to make some concessions to get the people I needed. Midship Campanile would only come if she could bring little Perilous here."

"Sure, and when people flat out turned you down you just kidnapped them anyway."

It had not occurred to Cass that there may have been adverse consequences had she declined this mission; having been in prison at the time, she had been in no real position to negotiate.

The man sighed. "It's good to meet you, Midship. Just limit the drake to the quarter deck, no sensitive areas please." The man picked up the drake, who immediately began nuzzling his neck with its snout. "Ok, ok." As he handed it back to the girl, Cass admired the drake's chitinous black scales with their iridescent green-blue highlights as they glistened under the corridor lights.

Commissar Nix noticed Cass' attention to them. "Miss Green, I see you've made it this far. Captain Chapman, this is Cassini Green, your pilot on this mission."

He extended a hand. "Nice jacket, Pilot. Pilot? Seems impersonal." He turned to Nix. "Is she ranked?"

Nix shook her head. "All non-coms are rated as warrant officers for Second Egress."

"Whatever. Doesn't matter. Think you can fly this old can, Green?"

"I can fly anything, sir."

"Sir?" He turned to Nix. "She's gunning for a commission already. I would, too, I'm sure the prize split is better."

"There's no prize split, Captain," Nix replied. "We really need to get to the briefing."

"I can walk and talk. I need to meet my new pilot. So, Warrant Officer Green, where'd you get that jacket? Floating in space junk?"

"No, it was my mother's. She was captain of the SFS *Victory*."

Chapman stopped smiling. "Amaranta Green? I...I didn't know your mother personally, but by her reputation she was one of the best."

"Thanks for not telling me to take it off because I'm a non-com, I get that from old Fed vets a lot."

"I know the feeling. Actually, this isn't my jacket, either. It was Captain Houlihan's, that's why it's maybe a bit big on me." They reached the ship's main hold. "Just so you know, Green, I have recently learned that half our crew is here against their will, so expect some unrest in the near future."

"Chapman!" Nix was supremely irritated. "Let it go, it was only three specialists. Ignore him, Cass."

"At your peril," Chapman muttered.

At the bottom of the nose ramp, the rag-tag group of strangers was met by an athletic woman with amber eyes and dark hair tucked under a Special Services cricket cap. Her all-environment coveralls were stained with soot, various industrial lubricants, and what looked like either Satsuman wasabi or guacamole.

"Looks like everyone's here. I am Lieutenant Commander Contessa Porvenir of the Satellite Federation. Welcome to Kestrel Base. I'm sure you have a lot of questions, I'd ask you to hold them until after you are briefed. That will happen once you are assigned quarters. If you'll follow me, we can do that now."

As they disembarked from the ship, Cassini could see that the walls and ceiling of the docking bay were carved from solid rock, meaning that they were likely inside one of Cartesia's moons or a nearby asteroid. Crews were moving work scaffolds alongside and over the *Pangolin*, getting ready to do...something. Off in the distance, to the front and rear, the docking bay opened out to space, and Cass noted the high concentration of asteroids outside; this rock was in the ring system. As they made their way to the freight lift, Chapman looked back at his ship with a concerned expression.

After taking the lift up a few levels, Commander Porvenir led them to a corridor that began an endless labyrinth of lava tubes leading throughout the facility. After a few minutes of silent walking through fluorescent-lit corridors of irregularly surfaced rock, Cass realized that the commissar and the captain had left the group. They reached a new corridor lined with countless doorways.

"You'll find your name on the door of your assigned quarters. Get situated and I'll be back in ten to collect you for the briefing."

The commander left them milling through the corridor, trying to find their names on the doors. Cass saw names that she didn't recognize; Lyonnais, Schultzenhausen, Fernandes. One name that did stick out to her was Moorcroft – Milt Moorcroft was the father of modern prismatic drive theory, which was the closest thing humanity had to a working FTL, even if it was still in the unmanned test phase. Heady stuff. And there were two Moorcroft rooms, meaning either the guy had his own suite or he'd brought Milt Jr., a prodigy in his own right. Nix was serious about recruiting experts, that was clear.

Cass eventually found her room. It was about as boring as one might imagine a room holed out of an asteroid would be. Carved rock walls. Bed. Refresh room. Climate controls. Comm system. Some lights. A closet for her clothing which, she found, also contained an exo suit; she assumed it was for a decompression emergency. The door chimed, and Commander Porvenir led her to the briefing.

As they entered the briefing room, Cass saw four people waiting for them. The first was the Commissar. Then there were two others, a blonde woman and a tall man in Hong-style dress, who both looked very familiar but she couldn't place them. The fourth was a Federation naval captain by the look of his red-jacketed uniform, who she eventually recognized to be Captain Chapman, from earlier. His bearing was much different with the uniform on; the Chapman at the front of the room was a serious man who would brook no disorder. She looked around at the group as they sat down. This was more than the group she had arrived with on the *Pangolin*, and there were quite a few surly looks coupled with crossed arms.

"I'll leave you to it," said Porvenir to the four at the head of the room as she left.

The tall man began. "Hello, everyone. My name is Kwan Li, Dauphin of the Hong Dominion Corporation. On behalf of

Representative Korovenko of Der Zweiwelten, we'd like to welcome you all to Kestrel Base, and thank you for volunteering to be a part of Operation Second Egress. Please watch this brief presentation."

The lights dimmed, and an old 2D holo projected on the wall behind the foursome. An older man in a lab coat was sitting on a stool in front of a clearboard with all kinds of mathematical calculations, formulae, and arc geometry on it. The holo was plagued with occasional artifacting and sound dips, indicating it had likely been restored from either poorly archived or deleted data.

"Hello," the man began, "I'm Dr. Cresh Bannerjee. If you're watching this, you've volunteered-" there were a few retorts and mutterings from the back of the audience at that, "to be a part of a grand experiment. Here at the Delft Institute, at the Novo Telemark, we began work on a project to map our stellar neighborhood. We've known the basics for centuries, of course, using a variety of telescopes from within our solar system. But we needed more than just locations of neighboring stars and potential exoplanets. Raw, detailed data on atmospherics, surface compositions. In short, what we're looking for are potentially habitable worlds. Not terraformable, but naturally habitable. Surprisingly, we are actually being co-bankrolled on this project by both Hong Dominion and the Runciter Corporation. I was as surprised as you are." Dr. Bannerjee stood and began walking stage right, as he continued his speech.

"The first order of business for Project Iditarod was to develop a probe capable of making a potentially infinite journey at incredibly high speeds, while also being able to collect and transmit the data we need." He stopped in front of a vaguely spherical metallic construction. "This is *Anchorage*, first of the Iditarod probes. Two-way ansible communication means it can be given redirect orders at any time, and we've worked with Rodriguez and Moorcroft on a stable

FTL drive. Maneuvering thrusters will work in vacuum as well as atmosphere..."

Somewhere during the presentation, Cass must have fallen asleep; her head bobbed, and she awoke as the lights were turned back up.

Cassini wasn't entirely surprised to learn that this was some kind of covert operation run by two of the system's greatest political mavericks. She was, however, surprised to learn that Project Iditarod was back in play. Her mother had mentioned it when Cass was young, and the idea of exploring the stars made her imagination explode with possibilities for much of her childhood, until pure piloting had become her primary focus.

Representative Korovenko stepped forward. "Operation Second Egress was a joint venture of Der Zweiwelten, Hong Dominion, and the Satellite Federation. Eventually, following the Scilla crisis, the operation was abandoned due to the signing of the Treaty of Kambei. The purpose of Second Egress was to make a focused effort to expand out to faraway star systems, establishing colonies and uncovering new resources."

Kwan continued, "Under the auspices of the Satellite Federation, a failed state whose few remaining citizens are no longer tied to any treaty, we are re-instituting the plan. When the Treaty was negotiated, the Frontier did not realize how far along the operation really was. Project Iditarod, those long-range FTL probes for mapping and surveying, were secretly launched just before the Treaty was signed. We have over 10 years of data that we can now send an advance team to verify.

"You will be that team."

Pause for dramatic effect. This guy was quite the politician.

Korovenko broke the pause at the optimum time. Power couple. "Commissar Helena Nix," Nix stepped forward, "will be leading the mission. Commanding the SFS *Pangolin* will be the Hero of the

Prahari Line-" Cass could see that the captain appeared very uncomfortable with that title - "Captain Maxwell Chapman." Chapman gave a small hand salute, but continued to stand at ease in the background.

"I'm sure you have questions," said Commissar Nix. "I suppose now's as good a time as any."

There were a lot of questions.

Cassini had a few, but she was sure one of these other subject matter experts would cover everything either in their questions or their answers. The initial questions – Can we go home? (No.) Ever? (We are preparing for a one-way trip.) Will we be reimbursed for our time? (Yes.) - ended when Korovenko made an impassioned speech about humanity's future, followed by a reminder that someday ships, cities, moons, planets, maybe even new elements or life forms would be named after everyone in the room. That shut everyone up real quick. It looked like it even impressed Captain Chapman.

After that, the meeting devolved from Q&A to unguided discussion in about three minutes. It was immediately apparent to Cassini that this was going to be a ship full of very smart people, most of whom didn't have a millimeter of common sense or field experience. Reps Kwan and Korovenko slowly extracted themselves from the discussion, leaving the captain and the commissar to try to guide the conversation as best they could.

After the first hour, in which they talked lab space (there would be ample), ship's atmosphere (standard ATMO5, which for some reason irked the climatologist), and food (makeit machines were all over the ship), they still hadn't gotten to anything remotely important. Cass interrupted the archaeologist (*why did we even need an archaeologist???*), who was complaining about his dual role as both mission archaeologist and ship's purser, with the first truly important question of the discussion:

"Do we get our own quarters?"

Captain Chapman answered her. "Well, like I said earlier, the *Pangolin* is an escort frigate, so it's built for a lot of possible uses. One of those is potentially carting around a lot of people. Each room on the quarter deck has an optional double bunk, but there are enough rooms that each of you will probably end up with your own quarters. However," he paused, knowing this was the "but" everyone was waiting for, "makeit stations and most refresh rooms are communal, not en suite. Is that the right term, en suite? Anyway, it's not a pleasure cruise, so you'll have to make do on that front."

"I don't care, as long as my lab is fully stocked with everything I requested," said the theoretical biologist, an impatient-looking middle-aged woman.

"If it's obtainable," Commissar Nix stepped in, "you'll have it. That goes for all of you."

"This isn't a generation ship, clearly," said an older man with a graying beard and a mane of silver hair, "so how are we getting out to the farthest reaches of the galaxy before I'm dead?"

"Were they not fully briefed on the mission details?" asked Chapman.

"They got the basics," replied Nix curtly.

"So, what is it?" asked the man. "Some kind of FTL, I'm guessing. Or jumpgates? Wormholes? Warp drive? Cryonics?"

"How old are you?" Campanile, the girl who owned the drake, asked the older man.

"Doctor Straightangle is fifty-three," replied Nix, "and probably the most over-dramatic man I've ever met. It's a good question, though. It's simple, really; the *Pangolin* is going to be fitted with an optimized prismatic drive."

Cass was suddenly concerned. "You know I've never flown anything like that before."

"No one has," chimed in Dr. Moorcroft, who had been very interested in lab space much earlier in the discussion, but from then until now had been lightly dozing in the back. "Nobody that's still alive to tell about it, anyway. We'll work with you on it, though."

A burly young man began to object. "I thought this ship was safe."

Cassini laughed. "You're about to go on an expedition into unknown regions of the galaxy and you're cacking on about safety?"

"Well, I figured we'd at least have a ship and crew who knew what they're doing."

Chapman stepped in. "The *Pangolin* isn't rated for FTL - what ship is? But the engineers are shoring up the superstructure right now. The thing I want to know is," he turned to Nix, "from where are we getting this drive?"

"You don't have the drive yet?" Dr. Straightangle asked.

"The Dauphin has promised to provide a drive from one of his R&D labs in the Belt," Nix replied. "But there is a catch.

"We have to steal it."

19

THE RUSTY SPANNER • KESTREL BASE • RING C • CARTESIA

Back when Kestrel Base belonged to Special Services, this level had been a transparisteel-floored mess hall where the Special Services patrol crews who patrolled MOE's patrol crews could watch their ships as they were overhauled in the gravdock below while they waited. Now, without official oversight, and with a patchwork of teams from around the League taking over the base, it had become an unofficial watering hole they called the Rusty Spanner.

There were a handful of makeit terminals to dispense food, but someone had the genius to put a bunch of broken cargo crates together and fashion a makeshift bar in the center of the mess hall. Coupled with half the lighting shut down to maintain a low energy profile, it made for a relaxing - if a bit rough around the edges - lounge in which to spend one's downtime.

Naturally, Max Chapman had nosed his way there, and had set up shop in a quiet corner with a good view of the ongoing refit of his ship. He'd have little to do beyond studying mission profiles for the next few tendays, until the *Pangolin* was up and running again and they could steal that FTL drive. Still, he'd talked a good game to Nix about easing off the brown stuff, so he was careful to nurse the Drumnadrochit on the small table to his left, next to the datapad he'd been studiously avoiding as he idly watched technicians replacing the *Pangolin*'s old Dyce .83 sublight drives with newer Aetherwerks .96s.

Just when he'd begun to bore of watching the mechanics weld thruster plating, Commander Porvenir entered the room and made a quick beeline for him.

"Captain."

"Commander. My compliments to your team, the repairs seem to be proceeding well."

"Thank you, Captain. We're on schedule for the moment, not a lot of wiggle room though."

"I'm sure you're all doing your best."

"Yes, sir." She paused the pause of an underling unsure if they've just been quietly dismissed. "Captain, do you have a minute?"

"Ship's not ready to go yet, is it?"

She smiled. "Not yet, sir."

"Then sit down, Connie. I'm off duty."

"In that case, I'll just grab a quick bite if you don't mind."

"By all means."

Porvenir returned from the makeit station with an aegean salad, and she sat across from the captain.

"I've been meaning to ask you," she managed in between bites, "we've got a lot of the old materials from Second Egress, someone found it all in an abandoned Special Services storage facility on Karaikal. I guess that's how a lot of this got started, really, finding that trove. That's where we found the Bannerjee vid, the probe frequencies and telemetries, there's mission patches, all kinds of stuff. I even found this swell hat." She tapped the brim of her black Special

Services cap, adding a smudge of feta to an edge already soiled with a variety of food residue and industrial chemicals.

"I was wondering where you managed to find that hat, it's not like Special Services to have a gift shop. Yeah, we'll have plenty of time to study all that once we're out in the black. Make sure all of it makes it on board."

"No problem, sir." She poked at a leaf of kale with her fork, unable to immediately spear it. "I also had one other question," she said quietly, "off the record."

"Connie, this whole mission is off the record."

Porvenir wanted to correct him that the mission was, in fact, very much on the record, which was the entire point of using a nearly-defunct government for the exercise, but who knew how many of those Caledonian whiskies he'd already had. "Understood, sir. It's just that, well, this ship is not where it needs to be defensively. We've got those quantum missiles, which are a great help, but if we're going out into the black...we don't know what's out there. The Sanzoku could have wiped us off the map last time we saw them, and for all we know they could end up being the nicest guys in the galaxy."

"I don't disagree," Chapman said. "In fact, I've expressed similar concerns to our superiors."

"And?"

"Chain of command, Connie. Chain of command. The Dauphin wants a peaceful mission, so we keep the weaponry to a minimum."

"Tactically, it's an absurd position."

"Agreed. But the Dauphin is no tactician, and he appears to be firm on this point and unwilling to budge. We'll just have to do the best with what we have."

"Rocks and sticks might help."

"Well, I suppose we can always run away if we have to."

They sat in silence for a moment, watching as the mechanics down below hoisted the prismatic drive's socket cradle into the engine hold.

"You know, Connie," Chapman said, brandishing his datapad, "I've been trying to understand how this FTL drive works, and frankly I can't make head or tail of it."

In that moment, she was relieved to see Milt Moorcroft nearby getting a sandwich from a makeit station. Porvenir called him over to explain how his optimized prismatic drive theory would work in practice.

"The calculations are sound," Moorcroft repeated any number of times throughout their deeply technical conversation. Chapman liked the physicist, but concluded that he wouldn't truly trust the math until he'd personally survived it.

So engrossed were they in conversation that they failed to notice Midship Alessia Campanile, the new comms officer, as she arrived in the Rusty Spanner and marched over to Chapman's corner, abruptly downed the entirety of Moorcroft's barely-touched Cassowary & coke, slammed the empty glass on the table and nearly knocked Chapman's forgotten datapad to the floor.

Chapman, startled, looked from the glass up to the young comms officer. "Midship, aren't you supposed to be calibrating the new comms?" he asked.

"Oh, I was," she told him, loudly. "But we have a problem." She produced a datapad, handing it to him. "Do you know what this is?"

He looked at the datapad. It was a display of the area surrounding the base. Points of signal contact, in green, were arrayed mostly along two lines, with a few in random spots. As the display repeated on a twenty second loop, Chapman noticed a fleeting red point for barely a second as two green points passed close to it at opposing angles. "Looks like traffic control. Were you using Cartesia Traffic to run baseline tests?"

"Right. And I picked up this bogey in red, no listed flight path with CT. See how it only shows when the other two craft come near it? That's because it's been hiding behind a ringrock. Those two craft had the bogey pinned – it couldn't move left or right without one of the craft visually seeing it. It could only move up or down out of the flight plane, which took it out of the rock's magnetic shadow."

He nodded. "But only for a split second, which was long enough for you to catch it." It was good work; he was beginning to see why Nix was willing to allow this undisciplined young woman to bring her drake along. "Are we sure this isn't a ghost? A glitch?"

"I've run it through three times, it's not a glitch. And Tactical says it's not a sensor ghost." She grabbed Chapman's Drumnadrochit and began to gesture wildly. "If it's not a ghost, that means it's a ship. And if it's a ship, and it's right on our doorstep like that, it's not a friendly. They've probably already called in a Frontier fleet, and we're stuck here with the ship in pieces..."

"Midship," Porvenir replied calmly, relieving her of the glass before it ended up all over her, Chapman, Moorcroft, and their entire corner of the Rusty Spanner, "if we've got a hostile bogey on our doorstep, the last thing we need is a comm officer with her head in a latrine. Calm down, get a glass of water."

Chapman exhaled slowly. "Commander, let's get to Ops. We've got to report this to the Admiral immediately."

"There it is."

The external security cams picked up a Frontier scout ship, popping down out of the magnetic shadow of a nearby asteroid for just over two seconds. The image sat frozen on the main display screen in Kestrel Base's operations center, which had been converted into a sort of mission control for Operation Second Egress.

"Ok," Admiral Vanakar began. "What do we know?"

"We know they know we're here," Campanile offered.

"No," Commissar Nix countered, "We know they know someone is here. We have no idea how long they've been here; they may think we're Belt pirates, or smugglers."

The Admiral shook her head. "We don't know how much they know. For the moment, let's assume the worst – but I'm not advocating acting on that until we get proof."

Chapman chimed in. "We need to accelerate our timetable. Porvenir, what's our current launch time?"

Commander Porvenir, patched in through the comm from the gravdock, paused as she checked her schedules. "Right now, we're looking at two to three tendays. Best time, without delays, is fifteen days."

"It's not going to take fifteen days for the Frontier to figure everything out," said Chapman.

"If we can get more repair crews, I can double-shift," Porvenir offered. "That would cut it down to about eight days."

Nix was growing impatient. "How many repair crews will you need to make that number thirty-six hours, Commander?"

Porvenir was taken aback. "Commissar, I don't think you understand. Welds need to cure, some of these installations can only be done in stages-"

"I don't think anyone here understands, Commander. If we ship in more repair crews, they'll see it. They'll report it. They'll send ships across the Kambei Line and all of a sudden this is an interplanetary diplomatic and mortal disaster, because under the treaty they're within their rights to cross the Line and attack any craft attempting to leave the system - with deadly force.

"Thirty-six hours is an optimistic guess, but let's go with it for now."

Chapman rolled his eyes. "We can't leave without the FTL, how are we going to get it in the next day and a half? The new sublights were just installed, the ship isn't even close to being ready-"

Porvenir interrupted him, "Sir, I'm checking my schedules and if I can get more repair crews, I can have sublights and basic life support ready. Comms and nav system are good enough, Midship Campanile can get those polished en route. All mission crew and materiel are present, I can get load-up started in spots where the repair crews aren't working."

"But no defensive systems." Chapman stated.

"We've still got the quantum torpedoes from the War, but we had to take the launchers offline to update the tactical core, such as it is. Basic laser batteries are due to arrive in nine days, but now I'm hearing this place will be a cinder by then."

"So, if we blow our cover and get more repair crews, we can get enough done to limp out of here," said Chapman, "but after that, where do we go? How do we outrun the Frontier without an FTL?"

Admiral Vanakar sighed. "I've been avoiding it, because it's not something I wanted to do, but the Dauphin said that if we ran into any trouble..."

"Midship Campanile, get me Lucas Wong. In the meantime, let's figure out what we can do about that scout ship parked outside."

20 |

REPRESENTATIVE
KOROVENKO'S QUARTERS •
KESTREL BASE

After the Noble Egress, the human race had come to the realization that there needed to be some changes to the way civilization operated.

Human life, it was determined, was valuable. Not just the preservation of the human race - a cryo chamber buried for a million years could accomplish that - but each and every human life, by virtue of its existence, from the most destitute vagrant to the Chief Executive of Hong Dominion, could make a meaningful contribution to civilization if given the chance. And in those days, when it was just Prahari, Der Zweiwelten, and Hong Dominion, there was peace.

Education and personal improvement were stressed. Violence had become almost completely nonexistent, except in the most lawless of ghettos like Mullvagrad and the Jade Quarter on (now long-gone) Phobos. Civilization had reached a peak, and while the Prahari Republic saw fit to ride this wave indefinitely, Der Zweiwelten and Hong grew decadent and bored. They both looked at the outer planets, with plenty of moons to colonize, tax, strip mine...

So began the Colonial Wars, a series of conflicts spanning over a hundred years which featured the first arms race since before the Noble Egress. But now, with the sickly, uninhabitable Yaodong a constant reminder of past mistakes, this arms race featured more conventional weapons: ballistics, lasers and the like against heavily armored starships. These battles were fought more to deplete the opposition's fighting budget than to deplete the opposition's fighting force. Casualties remained low, and respect for human life endured throughout the Wars, but even still, prolonged conflict had begun to take its toll.

The Sanzoku War, a decade after the last of the Colonial Wars (the Fringe War having ended with the Treaty of Kambei), had proven to be a major shock to the entire solar system. Thousands from all of the major powers were lost, by orders of magnitude a higher death count than anything since before the Noble Egress itself.

But now, if the reports were to be believed, people were killing each other in the Satellite Federation in the name of independence, using political excuses to act like a bunch of barbaric Belt pirates. The Fed was never a utopia, even at the best of times, but this was beyond the pale.

Darinka and Kwan had a plan. A new beginning for humanity. Leave the system behind, and once they got the infrastructure set up, anyone who wanted a fresh start could plant their flag.

Unfortunately, the Frontier was parked outside, waiting to blow the whole thing wide open before it even started. And for the first time since this operation began, Darinka was beginning to have real doubts about the plan's success.

She swirled the ice in her glass of Yekaterine & tonic, wishing she had a window to stare out of. Unfortunately, fate (or Admiral Vanakar) had placed her quarters ten meters deep in a ring rock.

Her door chimed. "Not now," she muttered.

The visitor knocked, and she recognized Kwan's usual pattern. She sighed. "Enter."

"I know I wasn't expected. May I?"

She plopped down in the room's only chair. "Why not?"

He approached cautiously. "I assume you've been briefed by the Admiral." She swirled her ice again, avoiding his gaze. He'd been here once before; he was in real trouble. "I'll take that as a yes."

"Li, I need to know this is going to work."

He smiled. "There was always an element of risk."

She sighed. "There's an awful lot riding on this. If it doesn't work, it could mean our careers."

"I've never known you to be so self-interested."

"Without my status, I can't help anyone."

"If anyone could find a way, you can." He sat on the nearby cot. "I've been thinking about a last-minute change to the plan."

"Now who's worried?"

He paused. "I'm going to join the *Pangolin*."

Darinka shot up out of her seat, shaking her head. "We have to execute the next phase of the plan together. The Executive, the Baroness...once word gets out, we need to present a united front in the Primary." His improvisational streak had gone too far this time.

"I'll talk to Chen when I go home to pack. And Admiral Vanakar's connected, she can help you with everything else. She'll probably be more useful to you than I could ever be. I'm no tactician."

"It's not the tactics I'm worried about." She began pacing, reconfiguring the plan in her mind. She wasn't thrilled about it, but she could improvise, too. "I'll talk to her. That means I won't see you again until we reach Anchorage One."

"That's true. We'll have planted the flag by the time you join us."

"The Hong Dominion flag?" she shot back, only half joking.

"Nice." He paused. She was owed an explanation. "The crew we've assembled is quite capable - Chapman's a military man who knows how to follow orders, and Nix will certainly keep the mission on track. But both of them have asked about weapons upgrades to the ship. I'm not sure they have a full grasp of what we're trying to do here, the importance of a pacifist mission. I think the team is missing...an aspirational leader."

"And I'm not aspirational?" She sat back down again.

"Of course you are, but we both know the next phase will never work without you in place, back home. With a few arrangements, it can easily work without me." Darinka wasn't sure this was completely true, but she could tell Kwan wasn't going to abandon this idea.

Kwan's datassist chirped. "Representative Kwan?" asked Campanile, her voice tinny through the datassist's comm.

"Yes?"

"Ten minutes to departure."

"Thank you." He stood. "Lucas Wong is here, he brought Mary. She'll give me a ride back home to pick up a few items."

"And talk to Chen," she forcefully added, making her way to the door.

"And talk to Chen," he replied, following her. "Next time I see you, it'll be on a new world."

As she leaned on the door jamb watching him walk away, she downed the last of her drink and hoped this would be the end of Kwan's improvisations.

21

OFS DAUNTLESS • THE KAMBEI LINE

"Now crossing the Kambei Line, Major," reported the *Dauntless'* first officer, a very no-nonsense man named Conroy. Major Sato much preferred him over the captain; Sakamoto was far too eager to please for her liking.

The major and Captain Sakamoto stood guard at the bridge's comm station. Unlike most other fleets, the OF's comms were unmanned; the ship's Taisei oversaw all communications operations. The Taisei monitored much more traffic in a second than a room of comm officers could even hope to parse in a day. This was one of the many advantages of being under the ever-loving gaze of Okaasan Heika.

Another advantage was the Taisei's ability to use frequencies outside of human comm ranges, encoding vocalizations at insane frequencies, and decoding them back again. It made for an extremely efficient, fully secure comm network. On the downside, bandwidth limitations meant that this secure network, known as the Tsushin, was 2D audio-visual only, and very short distance range. Had they not been broadcasting into such hostile territory, the major and the captain would have attempted to contact Captain Day from the ship's Proscenium.

"*Shoji*, this is Captain Sakamoto of the *Dauntless*. Please respond."

"Are you sure he's out here, Captain?" Major Sato asked, not bothering to mask the amusement in her voice, as he'd been repeating the same phrase ad nauseum for six hours.

"These are the coordinates of their last known trajectory," he insisted, flustered.

"*Dauntless*, this is *Shoji*. Captain Day reporting in," said a poor-resolution silhouette on the station's 2D display screen. "Sorry I'm late, but I've got some interesting news."

"Captain, this is Major Sato of the Shujutsu. I'm compelled to tell you that if I determine your actions are in direct violation of the wishes of Okaasan Heika Herself, you are to return with ship and crew for summary judgment."

The captain cleared his throat. "Major," he paused, "my distinct apologies. However, I think you'll be very interested to hear what we've discovered."

"You are overdue for crew turnover, Captain."

Captain Day sighed. "Operation Second Egress is back in play, Major."

There was a pause. It was a significant pause, because one of Major Sato's life's achievements was her success at scuttling Second Egress so many years ago. The pause froze Captain Sakamoto, his adjutant (far away at the ops station), and even Lieutenant Conroy in their positions. It wasn't often that an Outbound Fleet crew feared anything, but few crews had experienced Major Sato.

That the League of Worlds, or whoever was foolish enough to do this, was restarting Second Egress wasn't in itself a huge problem. The Kintsugi Nation had plenty of spies throughout the League;

they'd simply find out who was un-mothballing the Iditarod Project and destroy everyone and everything involved. The real issue was a political one - a shift in circumstances had made Second Egress viable in the mind of someone, despite the treaty-violating risks. A call to Envoy Stringfellow would appear to be in order, not to mention the Pontifex himself.

But first things first. "Come aboard the *Dauntless* immediately, Captain."

There was a small pause. "Begging the Major's pardon, ma'am, but under the circumstances that's not possible. I've got to maintain surveillance per my Taisei's orders."

"Captain," Sakamoto gingerly interjected before the Major ordered the *Shoji* destroyed, "this is Captain Sakamoto. Maybe you can explain your situation for the Major."

"We were sent to the Belt to restore Taisei access to the MOE's plexus network. We did that, but in the process we also found some valuable intel; over ten years' worth of the entire League's flight record data. Our tap to the plexus had only given us basic live flight data in real time, but these backups contain crew rosters, ship manifests, repair records, you name it."

"Impressive. And this information led you where?"

"Ma'am, our Taisei analyzed the data, including what the greater Taisei had missed when our tap was down, and sent us to the ring system of Cartesia, where a disused Special Services base looks like it's not so disused anymore. Lots of traffic in the last few days, especially. I saw a Federation ship fly in three days ago. I checked its profile; it was the *Pangolin*."

"From the Prahari Line?" Major Sato considered this. "You think they're trying to skirt around Kambei with a stateless ship?"

"Major, about an hour ago I made contact with a source inside the base who confirmed it."

"You have a source?"

"The source can only communicate in Morse static bursts to avoid detection, but confirms that this is, unofficially, a coalition operation to follow the Iditarod probe data."

"Taisei," Major Sato called with a surprising degree of urgency, "report status of signal Red Route One."

"Red Route One is currently transmitting on the HX band at a frequency of 45.3287, declining at an annual rate of .002." She nodded. That, at least, was still in place.

"Captain, we have three ships entering our XLR sensor field," the *Dauntless'* tactical officer reported.

"Can you get a profile, Ensign?"

"Ships are broadcasting as...SS...*Underpants*? And SS *Hard Luck Pony*. And another not broadcasting at all."

"Those would be the Belt pirates we saw coming into the base yesterday," said Captain Day. "I'd be very interested in where they're headed next."

"Agreed," said Major Sato. "Captain Day, return to your surveillance. See what else you can learn from your source. Captain Sakamoto?"

"Pursue the pirates?" he asked with a giddy smile.

She sighed, silently wondering which Outbound Fleet admiral had the unfortunate fate of being this man's brother-in-law. "Yes, Captain. Pursue the pirates."

"Ma'am, it appears the ships are splitting up, the *Hard Luck Pony* has broken off. Which do we follow?"

"Do we have an estimated heading for any of them?"

"The *Hard Luck Pony* appears headed for Hong Prime. The *Underpants* and Unidentified Contact Alpha have no discernible heading, ma'am."

"Whatever they're up to, they don't have time to lead us on a wild goose chase around the system. Follow the..." she sighed, "the *Underpants*, we know where the *Pony*'s going."

22

GALLEY • SS HARD LUCK PONY • EN ROUTE TO HONG PRIME

"So, Li, to what do I owe the pleasure?" asked Boxcutter Mary, Captain and Head Chef aboard the SS *Hard Luck Pony*. Kwan could barely hear her with her head inside a rather large commercial-grade refrigerator.

"If I told you, you wouldn't believe me," Kwan replied to her posterior.

She extracted herself from the fridge, her arms full of neck steaks neatly wrapped in white industrial paper and tied with twine. "You'd be surprised," she said, dumping the contents of her arms onto the cutting counter. "Got these off a transport bound for Hyperion," she told him, cutting the twine off the bundles with her namesake tool. "I was saving them for a special occasion. I think a state dinner qualifies."

"Mare, I'm not here in any formal capacity-"

"Be a dear and get me the Cerigan mine salt. It's in the cabinet behind you." The Dauphin searched the cabinet she'd indicated. "Second shelf down," he found it, "there you go." He handed her the grindshaker. "Here, throw away the wrapping while I salt these." The Dauphin collected all the twine and paper, and dropped them into the nearby incinerator chute, while Mary salted and continued, "My crew think very highly of you, Li. Doesn't matter where they're from. I've got people from Mullvagrad, even topside Cerigo; some from the Fed, or whatever it's gonna be; I've even got a guy from Satsuma, believe it or not. But a lot of my crew are contracts. They speak very highly of you, but Executive Chen is a different story. Sounds like you've got some PR issues at home."

He watched as she produced a prepknife from somewhere in the folds of her apron and began carving the brachiosaur vertebrae out from the center of the steaks. "Yes, well, people are entitled to their opinion."

"I guess my question is," she asked, pointing a very bloody knife at the Dauphin of Hong Dominion, "are you going to do right by your people? And by your people, I mean the people who were specifically created by your company to serve your company."

"It's a challenge, for sure. But let me ask you this: how many of the former contracts on your ship are viables?"

"Two, at least that I know about. The males almost never find out without testing. Or, you know, experience."

Kwan looked stricken by the very thought. "Yes, well...there are almost five thousand viables on Hong Prime alone, at least that's what the underground tells me. Rough estimates say another two hundred on Gushenxing. And we have no numbers on breeding outcomes, or if that's even happening on a larger scale. Or if it's even possible, really. I'm told I should prep for a colony of around three k total to start."

Mary disposed of the vertebrae and sinews in a simmering stockpot. "And what does the Executive think of all this altruism?"

Kwan sighed.

"You haven't told him, have you?"

"He'd probably have me executed."

"You're not wrong about that," she replied. "So, what are you going to do?"

"I'm not changing our initial plan. As soon as we find a world, Hong Dominion will have a protocol at the ready for choosing contracts to be colonists, and it will just happen to choose all viables. And if the official way doesn't work, I do have a contingency. The viables will have a good underground network with all the internal access they'll need to make it happen."

"I'm guessing...Corban?"

"He'll definitely be involved, yes."

Mary placed the steaks on a cast iron sheet. She then made her way to the wine rack. "And how does your partner in crime feel about all this?" she asked, selecting a dry red 332 Ioan Cellars that she'd liberated from the kitchen of a Hyperion luxury liner. Hyperians.

"She's made promises to some of the disenfranchised of her own people as well. But her biggest concern is not creating a worse version of the Frontier wars."

"You'd better be careful, Li." She popped the cork. "If you stop breathing that poison and take in some genuine air for more than five minutes, you might realize the Duchess is quite a catch."

"You sound like a rutting Frontier rube, Mare."

"They're a simple people, there's nothing wrong with that." She absolutely doused the steaks in red wine, then placed the tray into her Runciter Grillenmeister 9000 (which she had liberated from the galley of a Hyperion yacht). She took a pull from the bottle, and offered it to the Dauphin.

He shrugged, and took a few gulps. "That's...dry." He handed it back.

She replaced the cork, returned it to the wine rack, then made her way to the galley's comm panel. "Clark, can you get the case of Hyperion Oaks 318 from ship's stores?"

"Yes, ma'am," Clark replied from elsewhere on the ship. Did this pirate ship have a wine cellar? the Dauphin thought.

"So, how are you going to avoid the mistakes of your predecessors?"

"Well, makeit's come a long way in the past decade. We can basically build an industrial plant wherever we want and that would significantly cut down on the need for supply lines. And for the rest, there's FTL."

Boxcutter Mary's jaw dropped. "They didn't."

"They did. At least, Moorcroft says they did. He'd better be right."

She shook her head in awe. "I never thought I'd live to see it."

Li chuckled. "What are you, 50? Maybe?"

A small pirate, clad in the usual tatters, entered with a case of wine. "I'm not a day over 39, Dauphin," Mary said. She cracked open the case with a pry bar pulled, again, from somewhere within the folds of her apron. "Set the mess for a state dinner, Clark," she ordered. "Tonight, we feast."

Clark, whose helmet faceplate was adorned with the skull of some sort of bovine, nodded. "It's an honor, Dauphin," he said, and even though his voice was treated through the helmet's vocofilter he could tell the kid was fairly young.

"This is not an official visit," Li protested. He bent down a bit, conspiratorially. "Has the captain ever told you how she got into the business?"

The boy had become a pirate specifically because he hated pop quizzes. "I think it was a ransom job?" Clark ventured.

"I remember it like it was yesterday," Li said.

"It just about was, for me," Mary interjected.

"I'm telling the story! Admiral Maria Ximinez of the Hong Defense Force had stolen a ship and gone rogue. The HDF *Wellspring* was now the SS *Crimson Sail*. I just happened to have been on the *Wellspring* at the time, doing a naval tour as part of my curriculum. Your esteemed captain sent the Executive a ransom note, along with an image of me with a utility blade to my neck."

"Publicly, Chen would never admit to paying off rogue pirates, but he did, immediately," Mary added. "The way I've always seen it, the Executive has one weakness: you."

"That's ridiculous."

"I've seen it in his eyes when he talks about you. I saw it first hand when I was with the HDF, I see it now in interviews. I think he loves you like a son."

"Chen doesn't love anybody, like a son or otherwise. Maybe he needs a hit of whatever you guys are breathing on these ships. Anyway, Mary and I split the ransom 50/50." He laughed, for the first time in a while. "I've been in business with pirates ever since."

The timer dinged; the steaks were ready. "Li," said Mary, "you never did answer my question."

"What question?" Li asked as he, unprompted, extracted the steaks from the Grillenmeister 9000.

"Why are you going home?"

"Why don't you have a makeit on board?"

"We eat real food on my ship. Now answer me."

"I'm...heading home to pack. I'm going on the mission."

"I thought you were going to oversee things from Kestrel Base?"

"I was, but what can I say? Plans change." He smiled a politician's smile. "I guess my sense of adventure has gotten the better of me."

Maria Ximinez had known Kwan Li since he was a young palace page, and she was Fleet Commander in the Hong Defense Force.

She could think of many superlatives to describe him, but 'adventurous' was not one of them. Clearly, he was playing this one close to the vest. "Will you need a ride back to Kestrel, Li?" she asked the Dauphin.

"No, I'll be riding back by myself."

Clark, sensing his superfluousness to the conversation, excused himself. "I'll, uh...I'll set up the mess for the state dinner."

The Dauphin shook his head. "This isn't a state dinner, kid. Mary, I told you-"

She waved the bloody prepknife in his face again; a long, pink brachiosaur sinew swung limply from the sharp tip. "Let me have my fun," Boxcutter Mary replied.

23

SS UNDERPANTS • EN ROUTE
TO ASTEROID CX 218-239YG9

Cassini stared out the starboard viewport of the pirate ship's bridge, wondering how she had ended up here.

Sure, she could pilot anything. In space, in atmo - she'd even had a bit of experience under water. She had complete confidence piloting anything with a Z-axis. She could handle herself well in an old-fashioned donnybrook, for sure.

But here she was, on a ship with a stated mission of instant death in the name of profit, surrounded by the most uncivilized people in the solar system: Belt Pirates.

With their exo helmets adorned with the most vicious skulls their artists could imagine, and vocoders to mask and deepen their voices into obscurity. With their ever-sharpened knives to slice open the exo suits of innocent freighter crews before spacing them, or to cut their tethers to leave them floating free in the endless cold of space. These pirates were legendary for making killing an art form, all in pursuit of the almighty daric.

Teaming up with pirates to steal an experimental FTL drive was never on her list of future personal achievements. Yet here she stood on the bridge of this outrageous derelict as it tore through space at a speed best described as "unwise."

She noticed a framed certificate on a nearby wall. Upon closer examination, it appeared to be some kind of an official document issued from the Hong Dominion Corporation. The text was calligraphied almost to the point of unreadability, but she made it out to be a Letter of Marque and Reprisal. Basically, a license from Hong to traverse the space lanes and prey on any unlicensed independent operators. So, these weren't actually pirates, strictly speaking. They were privateers, loyal to Hong.

Though she had no doubt their loyalty could be bought by any higher bidder with less interest in official permits.

Between the ever-shifting sands of their allegiances, and their long-held reputation as the great bogeymen of space, Cassini was now beginning to realize that pirates were as much about keeping up appearances as they were taking your ship, cargo, sanity, and life, possibly in that order. She'd managed not to run afoul of them for most of her hauling career, though she'd met a fair number of colleagues who'd barely survived their unfortunate encounters. Based on her experience today, Cass had to admit that she wasn't all that impressed. She was still disgusted by their amoral reputation, but the feeling around the ship so far had been...friendly? Cooperative? Congenial?

One of the pirates approached her. Like all the pirates she'd met so far, this one was sealed in a patched-up exo suit accessorized with tatters of actual clothing; the fierce skull painted onto his(?) mask was an impressive work of art. "Ma'am? The captain will see you now."

Captain Wong had been asleep when she'd boarded, and in various comm meetings with the other ships in his pirate fleet for the last few hours. So she'd waited, studying the mission specs and wandering around the SS *Underpants* – an infinitely silly name for a ship covered in Hanzi threat graffiti, skeletons haphazardly lashed to the hull, and weapons both laser and projectile – idly trying to get a sense of how these people operated. So far, all she could tell was that they were very interested in edged weapons and, based on the smell of the exo suits they wore full-time, they were decidedly less interested in personal hygiene. Also, they had some talented (but possibly disturbed) artists on board to personalize the crew's gear for maximum ferociousness; and she couldn't tell if some of the metal surfaces on the ship were rust-colored or just rusted.

The pirate led her to the nearby Captain's Wardroom, behind the bridge area. As the door creaked open (dropping a few flakes of rust from the hinges onto the deck, solving one hours-old mystery), she was immediately met with a gaseous cloud of cologne. Standing at a portside bookcase was a man dressed, not in an exo suit, but a black naval jacket. He pretended to be casually reading one of the antique hardbounds from his collection. He was either illiterate, amazingly superliterate, or lacked attention to detail; the book he held, Dhaljit Singh's *The Fan and The Bellows*, was upside down.

Wong "suddenly" noticed Cassini after a few beats. "Ah! So this is the pilot I've heard so much about!" The dashing, mustachioed pirate clapped the book shut (which released a small puff of dust) and returned it to its place on the shelf. "Welcome aboard. I'm Lucas Wong, Space Pirate. I trust you've been treated comfortably. The Dauphin has told me you've been briefed, but I'm sure you have some questions."

Her "briefing" had consisted of a walk-and-talk from her quarters on Kestrel Base to the SS *Underpants*, led by Commissar Nix, in which Cass was basically told that the *Underpants* would take her to a secret Hong lab in the Belt where the experimental FTL craft was being developed. She would steal it and fly it back to the base, and the *Pangolin* would take off for infinity once the drive was installed. She was given a datapad with the necessary specs for the craft, a pair of welding goggles for some reason...and that was it. "Well," she began, as he directed her to a threadbare couch looking out over an aft view of the retreating infinite blackness behind the ship, "I was hoping that we would run a few practice simulations to iron out some of the details-"

Captain Wong shook his head. "I agree that we could use more time to plan, but this entire operation is out of time. The Kintsugi are out there, right now - you can almost see them," he said, pointing out the viewport dead astern, "following us at a discreet distance. We're pushing our engines to get out to the CX lab as soon as possible, and to work out some extra distance from their ship to buy the operation some time. We get you in, you get out with the FTL, you go back to the base. That's it. Are you going out like that?"

"Like what?"

"We can set you up with at least a chestplate, something tactical, yet streamlined, to fit under your flight jacket. Consider this: we've already shipped the lab staff to Kestrel to expedite your ship's refit, so ideally, we should be strolling into an empty building, no fuss. But if the Kintsugi catch up to us before we can get you to the test craft..."

She could handle herself in a brawl, definitely, but military-grade firefights were not her thing. "Some armor sounds good," she admitted.

"Have you eaten? I'm not sure there's time for a full meal, but we can get you something for after the ride down."

"No, I ate in your mess an hour or so ago." Stewed 'tops & muenster cheese. Mess was the right word for it, for sure. "Wait, what do you mean no time? When do we reach the lab?"

"Current speed, nearly half an hour."

She shook her head. She'd gone over the specs a million times over the last few hours, but her concern was the pirates' plan to get her to the ship. "I thought I'd have more prep time..."

"We all did, my dear. Gary is down on Deck 3, he'll provide you with some gear. Then meet me on the flight deck, the drop team should be ready by then." He stood, extending a hand. As she rose from the couch, she shook it definitively. "Between us, I was worried when they said they were putting a citizen on this. No offense, but in our experience they're not exactly the most courageous bunch."

"You just get me to that ship; I can handle it from there."

A voice on the ship's comm interrupted Captain Wong's reply. "Cap, short range contact Frontier One has increased speed to .9, should we match?"

"Good question." Wong frowned. "Engine room, can we hit .9?"

"We're topped out, I'm half surprised she hasn't flown apart already."

"Cack...get us whatever extra speed you can, throw anything not nailed down out the airlock if you have to."

"Aye, aye," both the helm and engine room replied.

"Deck 3, Miss Green. Now."

It turned out that Gary was the ship's outfitter, supplying weapons, armor and other mission supplies to the pirates of the SS *Underpants*. He did indeed have a chestplate that fit Cass comfortably and was streamlined enough to fit under her flight jacket. She also picked up some knee-shin combo guards, and some low-profile elbow-forearm pads just in case. (Gary called them vambraces, but she wasn't sure that was technically correct.) What Lucas Wong, Space Pirate, had failed to mention was that these pads were not being provided to her gratis.

"Twen'y-seven darics," Gary said in his vocoder-processed voice as Cass was halfway to the door. She should have kept walking, but for some reason she turned back to Gary.

"Excuse me?"

"Whaddaya got, krona? Pesetas? Don't take none o'that Frontier scrip, no sir. Daric, krona, peseta."

"Pesetas? You get a lot of contracts on these pirate ships?"

"Oh, we get everybody on here. But not for long." Gary leaned back on his stool, and resumed sharpening what looked like a pocket scimitar. "Wha's it gonna be, lass?"

Having come to the SS *Underpants* straight from Kestrel Base, and there straight from incarceration, it occurred to Cass that she had no durable currency of any kind. Her assets had been liquidated while she was in the Dom, and restoring her bank account was not part of the terms of her release. She hadn't been working for this operation long enough to claim her stipend yet.

She wished she could look him in the eye; the best she could do was look him in the gaping maw painted over the part of his mask where his entire face would be. "I've got to go save the human race. You can bill me."

She turned and left. As she charged out the doorway, the mini-scimitar clanged off the corridor wall ahead of her. She pocketed the knife, yelling back, "Clearly, you are not a professional!"

There were about eight pirates on the flight deck when Cassini arrived, plus Wong. The captain was handing out small stun pistols to the drop team, despite the fact that they carried enough cutlery to outfit a Shirazi slaughterhouse. "Ah, Miss Green. I don't suppose you have an exosuit with you?"

Cassini looked around the flight deck and realized something critical was missing: any kind of landing craft. "No...we're not gonna-"

"Yes ma'am, you are. I don't have time to explain-"

"Two minutes to drop," stated a voice over the ship's intercom.

"Well, all right, I have enough time to give you the Kintsugi version." Short and simple. Wong rummaged through some nearby crates as he talked. "First, we don't have any landers because we had to leave them behind on Kestrel. Sending the repair crews out in our landers helped us cut our turnaround time in half, and leaving the landers behind lightened our cargo weight and improved our speed by .31c. Here it is," he exclaimed, removing a particularly ferociously-painted helmet from a crate. He checked the distinctive blue canister on the back. "Fully charged with the good stuff, none of that ATMO5 cack."

Cassini took the helmet, looking it over suspiciously. "Is this supposed to-"

"He can't hear you, he's on a roll," one of the pirates informed her.

"Second," Wong shouted as he climbed up on a crate and grabbed a two-handed ceiling handle, as if making ready to do a thousand pull-ups for the Federation Physical Fitness Challenge, "there wouldn't be time to effectively launch a lander before the Kintsugi would be able to blow it out of the sky. As I said before, they're right behind us. And third," he pushed off from the crate, swinging with his legs pointed straight out toward Cassini, the handle above him dragging open a hatch revealing a winch about twice as long as she was tall. He landed about a foot in front of her with the grace of a true showman. "This ship is an old tetherminer."

Alphium tethers, showing only slight signs of oxidation, dropped from the winch. The tether ends were fitted with foot harnesses. The pirates stepped into their harnesses as the intercom announced the one-minute warning. Wong, realizing that Cass was hesitant, began helping her into her harness.

"The harness is secured to the tether completely. Just place one of your feet into the stirrup at the end of the tether, hold the tether with both hands, and you're ready to go."

Cassini was numb. She had done a few high-altitude jumps for fun. She had been out floating in the ether countless times. But never had she given thought to jumping out of a spacecraft in order to land on the ground. Who would even do that, and why?

Lucas Wong, Space Pirate addressed the drop team. "Pirates, you are some of the bravest crew I've ever served with. Have fun out there!" He gave them an exaggerated salute, then ran out of the flight deck.

"Ma'am," said the pirate to her left, "you should get that helmet on."

Cassini donned the helmet. As the neck seal tightened, the canister began regulating airflow. She inserted her right foot into the stirrup and, looking at the braided metal of the tether, put on her flight gloves before clutching it tightly.

There was a sudden rush of escaping air as the flight deck decompressed. The lights went out, and Cassini found herself floating off the deck as she became weightless.

"The asteroid's shadeshield will already be open above the lab," the pirate to her right shouted over the decompression alarms and the intercom countdown. "We should only be in open space for barely a second. The tether will do all the aiming." Though she couldn't hear it, she sensed a smile from the pirate. "We just hang on for the ride, ma'am."

Suddenly, she felt the tether stiffen. There was a loud CLANK above and behind her, followed by a small explosion.

And then Cassini died.

As abruptly as the tether shot down to the asteroid, it stopped. The whole thing was over in less than five seconds, which was just long enough to feel like an eternity. Cassini had no problem with the Gs; she still held the naval base simulator record (7.5) for five-year-olds at Ptolemy. But every experience she'd ever had was in a craft of some kind. Here, it was her openly exposed to the elements without even a jetpack to back her up, and, frankly, she was not a fan.

She'd kept her eyes closed tightly – involuntarily – so she missed the sights of the journey. She had heard the howls of the pirates around her, not knowing if they were screams of excitement or terror (it was excitement, for the record). She'd felt the tether in her hands go from a rigid metal bar to a slack rope again, the braiding of alphium relaxing even more as she removed her boot from the stirrup. She needed a minute to gather herself, she thought as she stumbled forward, then fell backward. One of the pirates caught her but, not anticipating her weight, he also fell.

The pirates removed her helmet. She was clearly unconscious.

"You got any smelling salts?" one asked.

"Do I look like a first aid kit?" replied another.

"Let's just get her to her ship," ordered the leader. "You four each take a limb. The rest take point positions, follow me."

Four of the pirates picked her up, making all manner of grunting noises.

"Really?" the leader asked. "She's not that big."

"No, but, she's surprisingly solid."

"Pants, this is Drop Team," the leader reported into the comm. "We're good here."

"Roger that, Drop," replied Lucas Wong. "Don't get captured."

"I sure wouldn't mess with her in a fight," the carriers continued complaining.

"It's not that bad. She's just solid, is all."

As the pirates carried Cassini inside the lab facility, the tethers retracted back up to the *Underpants.*

All the preparations had been made in advance. The facility was completely cleared of all personnel. Security doors were unlocked along the route to the hangar. The drop team knew the route intimately. The one thing they hadn't counted on was carrying the pilot instead of escorting her.

They were barely in the building when they heard the news they knew would eventually be coming, but they dreaded all the same. "*Underpants* to Drop One," Wong shouted over the leader's comm through static and the sounds of space battle. "You have incoming!"

Thankfully, Cassini was beginning to come around. The leader thought about consulting the mission datapad to make sure they were headed in the right direction. At that moment, the pirates ahead opened a pair of double doors, and the wall in front of them had a massive left arrow with HANGAR 1 in the usual variety of scripts.

"I guess we go left." This was from Cassini, to everyone's surprise.

"Ma'am, how are you feeling? Can you walk?"

"I think so." She tried it out and she could walk, barely.

"I hate to break this up," one of the pirates said to the leader, "but they're in the building."

The leader nodded. "You two help her. Let's go!"

With Cassini finally more or less mobile, they made it to the hangar in much better time. "Open the hangar doors," the leader ordered the pirate closest to the controls. "You two, help her into the ship. The rest, fan out."

The ship was roughly spherical, with recessed thrusters and a gyroscopic cockpit interior. The pirates sat Cass in the pilot's seat and harnessed her in. "Happy hunting!" they both said to her as they sealed the outer hatch.

Cassini tried to clear the cobwebs from her head and focus on getting herself out of here. She fed the coordinates for Kestrel Base into the navigational system, found the thruster controls, and started the launch sequence.

Outside, she heard muffled activity. She switched on the display and saw the pirates stunning the Frontier shock troops as they came through the doors into the hangar, and making a pile of freshly-stunned soldiers off to the side, likely to ransom after the battle was over. She switched the viewer back to a straight-ahead view, and wished she hadn't.

The Frontier shock troops were coming in through the hangar bay doors.

Pre-flight check was complete, but it would be another five seconds before she could get the green for launch.

She switched the display back to see how the pirates were doing. Now that they'd been outflanked, they were taking a defensive position around their ransom pile. A few of the pirates were down; the leader was on the ground, helmetless, and she wasn't moving.

Launch status turned green, and Cassini wasted no time. Using her thrusters, she took the long way out of the hangar, trying to knock down as many Frontier shock troops as she could on her way out. Once clear of the hangar, she aimed upward at top thruster speed. As she flew through the shadeshield gate, she noted that the *Underpants* had positioned itself between the gate and the Frontier's dreadnought to cover her escape, and was paying a heavy price for doing so.

The asteroid's gravity well was small, so she was out of it within barely a second. The navigational computer chirped; it had plotted a solution. Cassini activated the experimental drive, and died for the second time in the last half hour.

24

OFS DAUNTLESS · IN ORBIT AROUND ASTEROID CX 218-239YG9

Major Sato studied the tip of a massive harpoon that had pierced the hull of the *Dauntless* - in the washitsu of her quarters, of all places. The pirate weapon was one of six which had bored its way through the hull plating using glide-tipped power augers, and once the shaft had pierced through to the ship's interior it produced three grappling claws to secure the harpoon in place. The pirates had used the tethers attached to the harpoons to reach and, once they'd cut open a few entry holes, board the ship.

All of this was incredibly foolish, but, admittedly, effective. The Major didn't know how many pirates crewed the SS *Underpants*, but she knew there were currently 43 of them in the brig.

"Fascinating," Captain Sakamoto said, reaching out and rubbing a bit of oxidation off the harpoon shaft near the power auger, which had finally stopped idly spinning.

"Captain," ordered the Major, who had had more than enough of this feeble idiot, "get this out of my cabin. Repair this and the other harpoon holes. But first, have Lucas Wong sent to your wardroom. I want hourly reports on the repair status."

"Yes, ma'am!" She was out the door and halfway down the corridor by the time he could get the acknowledgment out of his mouth-breathing, sycophantic face.

It would take her three minutes to get to the wardroom next to the bridge. There was no reason Wong shouldn't be there by the time she got there herself. Let's test that theory, she thought as she made her way through the dreadnought's endless maze of lifts and corridors to the bridge.

The battle itself, such as it was, had gone fairly well for both sides; the pirates bought enough time for the experimental craft to get away, and the Kintsugi Nation now had 43 new prisoners. If the pirates had no intelligence value, they could always paint them up and send them to the second-hand auctions on Gushenxing, or just press them into bonded service of the Outbound Fleet like in the old sailing days. Okaasan Heika always said that the greatest joy was the joy of servitude, so why deprive these barbarians of said greatest joy?

The ship had sustained some damage, however, mostly from the pirates using their pokers and can openers on the hull. One of their harpoons had pierced the upper thruster configuration; engineering crews were working on it, but the fact that they'd have to keep their drive systems shut down during the repairs would slow their pursuit at a critical time. On a brighter note, the pirates' drop team had only stunned about half the shock troops she'd sent down to the asteroid, and a few had sustained second-degree burns thanks to that maniac pilot, but there were no serious consequences to speak of, Heika be praised.

As she entered the bridge, Lieutenant Conroy saluted and reported the ship's status. "Major, we're currently ten hours from Cartesia, Engineering estimates we'll be able to double our speed in three hours, once initial thruster repairs are complete. The Bastion is aware of our situation, and," he swallowed nervously, "due to the extreme importance of our mission Okaasan Heika has authorized the nullification of mortal safeguards."

This was not a small detail. The Kintsugi Nation rarely agreed with the rest of the solar system, but Okaasan Heika, probably in remembrance of so many of her contemporaries lost in the famines and plagues during the Colonial Wars, had consistently maintained the high regard and respect for human life that was shared by the other governments. "Thank you, Conroy."

"Also, ma'am, your guest is awaiting you in the wardroom."

She nodded and headed for the wardroom. "As you were, Lieutenant."

Lucas Wong was flanked by two shock troopers and manacled to a chair, yet he seemed to care about neither of these things. Instead, he was fully engrossed in the view outside the wardroom's porthole.

"You are the captain of the ship that attacked us?" Major Sato began.

Her question broke his reverie. "What? Oh, me? No. Certainly not."

"The ship you were on took a parallel position to the *Dauntless*, attacked the ship with harpoons, and your boarding teams made quite a mess."

"Well, I was a passenger, on my way to Kepler, and the captain made some announcement about an unscheduled emergency side trip..."

"You were seen leading one of the boarding teams. Comm traffic indicates that you, in fact, coordinated the boarding teams. According to League security records, you are Lucas Wong, a notorious pirate with a million-krona bounty on your head from Der Zweiwelten."

"No, no, no, you've got this all wrong...it's two million."

"The Kintsugi Nation's relationship with Der Zweiwelten is not amicable at the moment. Maybe you can help us smooth things over."

"I have trouble believing they'd drop two million krona on me right now, while the Cosmoflot is still just a couple of tugs and a billion tons of lusitanium ore. They've got bigger fish to fry than little old me."

"Do tell, Captain."

"I'm just saying, they're pretty busy trying to rebuild after the War, I mean, that's no secret. I keep up with the bulletins, but if I had any special insights I wouldn't be tied to this chair, right? Right?"

"Were you aware that there's also a price on your head in our territory?"

"What did I ever do to Okaasan Heika and Her fine children?"

"Theft and resale of Blue ring any bells?"

Wong was taken aback. "We have an existential right to clean air."

"On that point, we agree. But you need to pay for it like everyone else."

Sato would have to try another tack. Even shiftless Belt pirates were reasonable when it came to survival. "I should tell you that I've been authorized, in this situation, to use mortal force to complete my mission."

"'Mortal force'? Are you threatening me? I'm Lucas Wong, Space Pirate. I'm captain of a mercenary fleet the likes of which the system has only dreamed about in its darkest nightmares. I've been in worse jams than this."

"Do you know what our plan is?" Sato asked, sitting in front of him on Captain Sakamoto's desk so she'd be more relaxed, and he'd have to look up at her.

"No, but I have a feeling you're gonna tell me and I'm probably not gonna like it," Wong replied, with more than a little bit of edge in his voice.

"We're on our way back to that ringrock at Cartesia. You know the one. And when we get there, we're going to blow it up. Unless you can give me a reason not to."

He should be ready to bargain now, she thought. "Listen, I don't really know anything." He laughed nervously. "Ask anybody, I'm a walking imbecile."

"That much is certain." She jumped down from the desk, only to sit behind it. Now she was more distant from him, but at eye level. "If we destroy that rock, people will die. Who knows, they may even be innocent people. The Kintsugi Nation will be well within our legal rights to do this. Unless you can tell me a compelling reason why I should hold back the wrath of Okaasan Heika herself, I don't see why I shouldn't just blow every single one of you pirates out an airlock."

All this talk of murdering innocents and airlocking his crew was getting to him. "Look, I had very limited exposure to any of the plans. My job was to get the repair teams to the base, get the pilot to the ship, and slow you guys down. That's it. I don't even know what the point of it is. I mean, for me, it was the money."

"So, you don't know where that ship is going?" she asked.

"I never thought to ask."

She was satisfied with this answer. "I believe you."

"Good! Good." He began to relax. "So, if you believe me, you won't airlock my crew, right?"

She smiled a predatory smile which, it occurred to her in that moment, she hadn't used in years. "We'll see."

25

DAUPHIN'S RESIDENCE • IMPERIAL PALACE • HONG PRIME

The Dauphin and Chamberlain Fong were in the dressing room, packing a garment bag, when Executive Chen bounded into Li's residence flat, red-faced and trembling with rage.

"This has gone far enough! I have given you a very long leash, I have trusted that you are acting in the best interests of the Corporation-"

Kwan, undistracted from his current task of choosing tasteful activewear for his upcoming adventure, replied without looking back at Chen, "Your trust is not misplaced, Executive."

"At the moment, it is looking very misplaced. Our experimental propulsion lab is on fire right now, that represents a massive capital expenditure loss! And Stringfellow is on the comm accusing us of plotting to break the Treaty of Kambei? The sanctions alone could cripple the corporation for generations – what if they decide to break up the operating companies? Have you thought of that?"

"Our new fleet is a few months from ready, which is about a year sooner than anyone else in the League. Let them try to break up

HD when we've got ten new *Ming*-class destroyers parked around our orbit."

"Oh, you have thought of everything, I see. And what if the Frontier has more ships than they're letting on?"

The Dauphin sighed. "They don't."

"My lord," Chamberlain Fong interjected, "perhaps once you've calmed down, this conversation can continue in a more civilized way."

"Fong..." Executive Chen gave him a sidelong glance. "I want to know right now, Li. Why all this risk?"

"I know a lot of things, Executive. I know about ATMO5. Actually, I think I know more about ATMO5 than you do. And I know that we're running out of time."

Chen paused. "They will figure out a cure for the Roga."

Kwan finally turned his attention away from his racks of clothing. "It's more than just the Roga, but even that – the Kiteri Roga is inexcusable. We deserve to be litigated into oblivion over that."

"So, this is your way of punishing the company? Getting the Frontier to blow up one of our most promising achievements?"

"The technology is in safe hands. In fact, I'm going to meet with it now."

"You're not going anywhere...wait a minute, did you steal the drive?"

"I'm going to be gone for a while, Executive. When I return, our holdings will have increased exponentially."

"Our holdings..." Chen began to see where this was going. "You are going to claim new territory? Outside the system?"

"We aim to find habitable worlds that won't require terraforming, but I'm sure we will also find plenty of rocks out there for you to strip mine."

"But the distance...our supply lines-"

"Will be short now that we have a functional FTL drive. Executive, the drive works. I've already worked it out with Moorcroft and directed Hong Astronautics to get production started." He packed the last of his activewear and closed the bag. "I trust you will care for the company with your usual deft skill until I return." And with that, he was gone.

"My lord," Fong bowed to Chen, "my apologies, but I feel quite strongly that I must accompany the Dauphin on this journey."

Executive Chen was taken aback. "Chamberlain, you have not been outside the palace walls in fifty years. You have never even left the planet, as far as I know."

"My feelings are surprising even to me, my lord. But they are exceptionally strong in this matter. Please forgive me."

"I understand. You continue to serve your house diligently, Fong. There is nothing to forgive." Executive Chen could not imagine what dangers would await them. Chen was a man of action, but his world was one of balance sheets and fiscal targets. A long, long way from where Kwan was going. "Chamberlain, please take good care of the Dauphin."

"It is my honor, my lord."

26

MEDBAY · SFS PANGOLIN · KESTREL BASE

The disused medbay at Kestrel Base had been converted into overflow barracks for repair crews, so Cassini had to report to the *Pangolin*'s medbay to be cleared for duty. After her little FTL trip, Chapman had decided that it would be a good idea to make sure the pilot hadn't been completely addled by the process. Doctor Abdelaziz was conducting a quick brainscan when Chapman arrived for the report.

"Doc, how's our pilot?"

Abdelaziz nodded. "All checks are reasonably within her baseline. A few elevated chemical levels, likely from the experience of traveling past the speed of light, I'd imagine, consistent with Moorcroft's data. Physically, she's cleared for duty." He slapped Cassini on the back, smiling. "Get out of my medbay!" She smiled back weakly, hopping down from the exam table.

Cassini was quieter than Chapman had remembered her. "Come on, pilot. I'll walk you to your quarters."

"Ok," Cassini replied. But he could tell she was miles away.

As they left the medbay, Chapman tried to start a conversation. "So, we've had some fun while you were gone. Preparations are proceeding at breakneck pace. Did the Belt pirates treat you all right?"

Cassini didn't immediately reply. Chapman gave her time; he wasn't afraid of a little awkward silence. Eventually, she came out with: "Cap, I don't want my assigned quarters."

Chapman didn't particularly care what quarters she had, though they had assigned her one near the command deck for quick access. "Is there a specific quarters you had your eye on?"

"I want to stay in the cockpit full time."

Chapman considered this. "Well, I'd have to clear it with Abdelaziz and Commissar Nix. It's not really set up for that kind of thing, though. There's a mini-makeit but it's very basic, I know personally I didn't find the chair very comfortable, there's no plumb-"

"I'll figure it out, Cap. I just need to be up there for a while. FTL travel is...I just need to figure it out."

Chapman stopped her mid-stride. "What happened to you out there? Look, I need to know if you can do your job-"

"Right now, the only thing in the universe I'm confident of is my ability to fly this ship, lightspeed or otherwise. It's everything else that I need to get settled."

Commander Porvenir came charging down the corridor with a few meters of coiled triaxial line. "Coming through. Make a hole!" Chapman and Cassini let her pass between them.

"As you can see, things are a bit busy at the moment," Chapman told Cassini apologetically. "Look, I just need to know that I can count on you when the time comes."

"I'm here for you, Cap. You need this ship to move, just say the word."

"Good. I'll talk to the doc and the Commissar about you staying in the cockpit full time, but you have my permission to set yourself up there for now. You're, uh, excused from repair work for the time being. Just be ready to go within the next few hours, ok? Dismissed."

"Aye, Captain." Cassini headed toward the command deck, a ghost of her former self. She probably just needed time to process everything. Unfortunately, time was a commodity in very short supply.

The intercom chirped. "Captain Chapman to the gravdock. VIP arrivals." That would be Mission Benefactor Kwan Li, here to join the crew. Having the Dauphin on board, Chapman gathered, was not part of the original plan. As near as he could tell, the Dauphin would be using his presence and stature as a shield, to prevent the Frontier from destroying the *Pangolin*. They wouldn't dare take out the heir of Hong Dominion, treaty violation or not.

He hoped that logic held.

OFS SHOJI • OUTSIDE KESTREL BASE

Captain Day stewed, arms crossed, in his bridge station as the tac display showed the Hong cutter *General Chang* landing at Kestrel Base.

"Cack."

"Ten demerits, Captain," reported the Taisei.

Grafael Day had spent much of his career avoiding attention. He was careful to accept only the most boring postings. He turned down promotions until they were basically forced on him. But Okaasan Heika had never forgotten about him; she never forgot anything. For his sins, she'd put him in a position where, at best, he'd be a footnote to history. At worst, he'd be forced to start another war, this time with mortal stakes. *We're all her puppets*, he mused ruefully. *She pulls our strings and we have no choice but to dance.*

"Taisei, any orders from the Tsushin?"

"Negative, Captain. No Imperial ships within Tsushin range. OFS *Dauntless* still inbound, arrival in range: one hour thirteen minutes."

"Caaaaaaaaaack."

"Ten demerits, Captain."

"This is one of those times I'm glad I only pull a colonel's salary," offered Keyes helpfully.

"We've seen overloaded landers dock there, we've seen an experimental craft come howling into the sector at 1.2c and fly into that installation. Now we have the personal craft of the scion of one of the League's great powers flying in like he's running late for a board meeting. I feel like we've got more than enough probable cause for action per Kambei."

"Taisei, can we override silent running to contact Gorobei about a violation of the Treaty of Kambei?" Keyes asked.

"Negative, silent running can only be overridden by command from the Bastion."

Keyes shook his head. "Which we're not going to get relayed to us until the *Dauntless* arrives."

"And by then it could be too late. Cack!"

"Ten demerits, Captain."

"Taisei, do I have the authority to negotiate with opposing powers until orders are received from the Bastion?"

"Yes, Captain. You have authority to act as proxy until overriding orders discontinue diplomatic efforts, or ranking diplomatic officers can continue efforts."

"Graf, can't you wait it out another hour?"

"Another hour and they could be gone - I could get court-martialed for dereliction by inaction."

"Well, it's your decision, Captain."

"Thanks." Captain Day sat up in his seat, cleared his throat, and pressed the comm. "Unknown facility, this is Captain Grafael Day of the Outbound Fleet Ship *Shoji*. I am requesting...parley pursuant to," he checked the Treaty on his text display, "Section 7, subsections 1 and 4 of the Treaty of Kambei. Please respond."

"Heavy is the head that wears the crown."

"Shut up, Chuck."

"Five demerits, Captain," the Taisei reported.

A response came through on the comm. "This is Admiral Jemma Vanakar of the Satellite Federation. Please dock at the north polar hatch. No weapons, please."

"Understood." Captain Day exhaled a breath he hadn't realized he was holding. "Come on, Chuck. If I've gotta do this, I'm dragging you with me."

"Cack."

"Ten demerits, Colonel."

28

NORTH POLAR AIRLOCK •
KESTREL BASE

The women stood at the airlock entrance, waiting for the Frontier spies to arrive.

"Do you really think they'll come without any weapons?" the Duchess asked. This was a much lower level of negotiation than she was used to. Almost thrilling, in its way.

"Would you?" Admiral Vanakar countered.

"They'd be in violation otherwise," Nix pointed out.

"Right, but do they care? If they think we're in violation, they could interpret-"

The ceiling airlock hatch opened, and two officers climbed down in their Frontier khakis and caps, a younger man with a captain's rank insignia, and an older man who looked to be a colonel. They stood at attention. "Captain Grafael Day of the Outbound Fleet Ship *Shoji*. This is Colonel Charles Keyes. On behalf of Okaasan Heika and Her Kintsugi Nation, we wish to discuss terms of the Treaty of Kambei which may have been violated by a person, persons or state entities aboard this installation."

Vanakar stepped forward. "I'm Jemma Vanakar, Ranking Official of the Satellite Federation. May I present to you Commissar Helena Nix of the Federation's Political Bureau, and Der Zweiwelten's Duchess Ravenscar, who is here acting as an impartial observer."

Captain Day seemed taken aback by the Duchess. Either he didn't expect an impartial observer to be present, or her ethereal beauty had his uncivilized Frontier brain rutting away in his imagination. "I...very well. There's a lot to talk about, so unless we're going to do it standing here..."

"Have you ever done this before?" Nix asked with a slightly predatory look in her eye.

"Well, I have...some diplomatic experience."

The goal now was to stretch these negotiations out as long as possible, until the *Pangolin* was ready to launch. Vanakar, who was the least diplomatically experienced of the three of them (and, therefore, the least intimidating), had elected to run point. "Please, Captain. Colonel. Let's go somewhere more comfortable where we can talk."

29

GRAVDOCK · KESTREL BASE

As Chapman made his way down the *Pangolin*'s nose ramp, idly wiping optic solder from his hands with a rag in preparation for a clean, formal "welcome aboard" handshake with the Dauphin, he noticed that the man walking a few steps behind Kwan Li looked...a bit ill? He was walking as if he was a human-shaped bag filled with rats pretending to masquerade as a person. Maybe Kwan was bringing some kind of performance artist along, but it definitely seemed amiss.

The Dauphin, steps ahead of the shambolic mystery man, seemed to have no idea what was happening behind him. "Captain Chapman!" he called out, still meters away from the *Pangolin*. "How soon do we launch?"

"External elements are as prepped as they're gonna be," Chapman replied, having a hard time concentrating with whatever was going on back there. "Crews are still hard at work on the inside, though. Is your man ok?" Chapman pointed to the trailing Chamberlain.

Kwan turned around, and ran to the man in panic. "Chamberlain!" he exclaimed. "Get a doctor, Chapman, quickly!"

Chapman ran back up the nose ramp and slammed the nearest Medic Call button, which would alert Dr. Abdelaziz to get out there as soon as possible. He hurried back down to help the Dauphin with Chamberlain Fong, who was now laying on the deck with the Dauphin worriedly at his side.

"My lord," Fong said in barely a whisper, "If what I believe is happening is actually happening, you need to kill me. Please. The mission is too important."

"He's delirious," Kwan told Chapman.

"You must understand," Fong countered, more forcefully now. "I don't think I'll be able to regain control..."

"Nonsense," Kwan told the aged Chamberlain. "Chapman, help me get him up, we can get him to the medbay."

"No."

The voice didn't belong to Chapman, or the Dauphin, or the Chamberlain. It wasn't Dr. Abdelaziz, either. The voice was female; resonant, if a bit tinny. It almost sounded piped in on a comm channel. And it came from the mouth of Chamberlain Fong.

"This base and everyone in it will burn." Judging by the Dauphin's reaction, Chapman deduced that this was not the sort of thing the Chamberlain was given to say. "I've spent the last hundred years trying to prevent people like you from crossing my territory. From leaving the system. Did the Sanzoku War teach you nothing? There are dangers beyond our system, unspeakable perils, and you just rush headlong into the jaws of destruction like it's a tenday camping trip."

Chapman, starting to fully catch on that this was an extraordinary event of some kind, asked the non-Chamberlain, "Who are you?"

"Once, I was known as Mitsuko Katayama. Today, I am known to my Children as Okaasan Heika."

"That's ridiculous," Kwan laughed humorlessly, "Okaasan Heika is a...a fiction."

The non-Chamberlain stood, and looked upon the Dauphin with eyes that showed nothing but panic as they searched for a way to communicate. It was clear that the Chamberlain was still in there, at least somewhere, still in control of his eyes at least. But his other movements and the words coming from his now twisted scar of a mouth were under the control of someone else entirely.

"The sins of the forefather return on the son. Your family has violated one of the most sacred laws the human race has. The great Cheng was a conceited fool, and it does not at all surprise me that he would be so bold as to invite abomination into his household and normalize it to the point where now, over a hundred years later, no one in your family even remembers."

"What does that mean?" Chapman asked. He hadn't felt this far out of his element since the Alan Bean Ballroom. "Dauphin, what is going on?"

Now that Okaasan Heika had full control of Chamberlain Fong's extremities, she began to pace, striding like a smilodon on the prowl. "This body," she stretched his arms as if awaking from a tenday slumber, "is older than any human can live, especially these days. Especially in an atmosphere full of that poison, ATMO5. But Fong is loyal beyond question, so no one questions. He hasn't aged a day since he turned a hundred and twenty, but you're all so busy with your balance sheets and your quarterly projections that you don't think about the kind old man in your midst. The only man you know you can trust.

"I did not want to do this. I did not want to waste my perfect conduit into the inner workings of Hong Dominion. But, despite what my Children would tell you, I am not infallible. A tip of the hat to you, Dauphin. You and the Duchess have kept me on my toes.

Well played, indeed. You've forced me to sacrifice my queen, but the checkmate is at hand. Goodbye, Dauphin."

Dr. Abdelaziz arrived at the top of the nose ramp with an emergency medkit just in time to see Chamberlain Fong faint dead away. Kwan caught him in his arms and lowered him to the floor.

"Doc, what is going on with this guy?" Chapman asked as the doctor analyzed Fong with a medical scanner.

"Vital signs look normal, a bit elevated...wait, his chest-" Dr. Abdelaziz put his hand to Fong's chest, "his chest is hot. Just radiating heat."

Fong's eyes shot open. He clutched his chest. "No." He stood up, backing away from the men. "I'm sorry. Just...when I get to the edge, open the force field and blow me out into space. It's your only chance, and even that is a slim one. I-I failed you, Dauphin. I'm so sorry. Please run!" He said that last part while running down the gravdock (at a speed much faster than Chapman would have expected from a man that old), his clothing now on fire, past the *Pangolin*, toward the portside gravdock entrance. Fong's stride began to falter as his skin began to melt off, revealing a cordrasteel endoskeleton that itself began to melt, so powerful was the heat emanating from his rib cage.

Humanity had, of course, banned high-intelligence computational programming after the Noble Egress, but not before androids had become a rare, prohibitively expensive curiosity for the rich. It made a twisted kind of sense that Hong would have kept one in its employ for all these years; what more exclusive item could there be than an android, and how better to hide one than in plain sight? Executive Cheng had been the most vain of all of Hong's heads of state, and his final mistake had now come to fruition, so many decades later.

It occurred to Chapman as they watched the android melting into slag a few hundred meters away that the reason the android was melting was that its small fission reactor (which was, for the record, so well-made that it hadn't glitched in nearly 150 years) had been sent into meltdown, presumably by Okaasan Heika. This meltdown would undoubtedly cause a small nuclear explosion. It also occurred to Chapman that Fong knew this, which was why he'd told them to blast him into space. A thing I should probably do as soon as possible, Chapman thought.

"Get on the ship," Chapman told the doctor and the Dauphin. "Now."

Chapman found the portside Emergency Decompression lever. The *Pangolin* and the *Chang* were moored securely, most of the important tools and equipment were already on the ship...he threw on the nearest safety harness, grabbed the emergency handlebar, and pulled the lever.

The force field discontinued, and the explosive decompression sent everything not secured straight out the portside gravdock entrance. What was left of Chamberlain Fong immediately stopped flaming, though it still glowed a volcanic red as it skidded past the threshold and into the cold, dark nothing of space.

And then it exploded.

Chapman watched as the shockwave pushed the *Pangolin* forward, breaking the ship from its moorings and skidding it further into the gravdock. The explosion shattered the rock around the portside entrance, causing a massive safety bulkhead to deploy right where the ship had sat only seconds earlier. The bulkhead would have bisected the *Pangolin*'s rear thrusters and destroyed any chance of the ship escaping.

The bulkhead seal automatically re-compressed the gravdock, or at least the two-thirds of it that was left, and Chapman unharnessed himself.

He'd already almost died on this mission and he hadn't even left the refit dock yet.

30 █

OPERATIONS CENTER •
KESTREL BASE

The shockwaves of the explosion were felt throughout the installation. All crew were already aboard the *Pangolin*, including base personnel, so the Operations Center was otherwise unmanned. Commissar Nix checked the base's systems to see what was going on down in the gravdock.

"I'm sure it was just some sort of chemical explosion," Admiral Vanakar explained to Captain Day.

"Maybe we should go check it out," Colonel Keyes offered.

"No, no need," Nix replied from the status terminal. "Looks like there was a fire in the gravdock, they had to perform an emergency decompress." She paused before continuing. "I should get down there, in case they need a hand."

"Agreed," said Vanakar. They exchanged nods, and Nix headed off to the *Pangolin*.

"Admiral, where is everyone?" asked Captain Day.

"What do you mean?" replied the Admiral. "It's a very small facility, it only takes a few crew to run it."

"So, you're telling me that a Federation admiral, her political officer, and Der Zweiwelten's League representative are just running this station by themselves?"

"I'm not telling you anything, Captain. You may infer what you wish."

Colonel Keyes and Captain Day conferred briefly, then Keyes left the room.

"Where's he going?" asked Vanakar. Day didn't bother to respond.

Captain Day was beginning to lose patience. He didn't want to be here in the first place, and yet here he was questioning a bunch of shady characters, all of whom were way above his pay grade. "And you, Duchess? What's your role in all of this, beyond staring at the ground and filing your nails absent-mindedly?"

Darinka said nothing.

Day looked up, closed his eyes, and prayed to Okaasan Heika for strength and discernment. "Look, I've got to tell you, if you're preparing to leave the system Okaasan Heika is going to have a big problem with that. And the more I look around, the more I think that's probably what you're trying to do here."

"Captain, this is a Federation refit installation in Federation territory. I'm not sure you have any reason to be here, but we've been nice about it so far. The longer you're here, the less nice I'm going to be —"

Vanakar was cut off by the sound of the proximity sensor. She called up the nearest display. A massive ship had arrived, parking itself in front of the starboard gravdock entrance.

OFS *DAUNTLESS*, the display read. FRONTIER TERRITORIES.

SFS PANGOLIN · GRAVDOCK · KESTREL BASE

Chapman reached the command deck just in time, as Operations was relaying the latest news to the ship via an open comm channel.

"Let's see it," Chapman ordered. The tac table image resolved itself out of millions of tiny points of light; it was the *Dauntless*, hovering just outside the starboard gravdock entrance (aka the only remaining way out of the gravdock).

Over the comms, they could hear the conversation between Admiral Vanakar and the *Dauntless*. "Unknown installation, this is Major Sato of the Kintsugi Nation. Please surrender and prepare to be boarded, per the terms of the Treaty of Kambei."

"This is Admiral Vanakar of the Satellite Federation. While I am aware of the terms of the Treaty, we have already been boarded by-"

"Campanile, can you cut off the audio?" Chapman asked, studying the *Dauntless* image.

"Aye, sir," Campanile answered, muting Vanakar's valiant stalling effort.

Commissar Nix arrived, joining Chapman at the tac table. "She's right in our way," Nix observed, indicating the new Frontier ship.

"Any way we could blow the bulkhead behind us, get out that way?" asked Campanile.

"We've still got quantum missiles in the munitions stores left over from the War, but launchers were taken offline for the refit," Chapman replied.

"Even if we did use the missiles, the bulkhead's collapse would probably further weaken the structural integrity of the base," offered Lt. Commander Porvenir from the tactical station. "The entire gravdock could collapse, crushing the ship."

"So that's a definite no on the bulkhead, then. All right," Chapman looked around at the command deck crew. "Do we have any other weapons?"

Porvenir shook her head. "This was never much of a warship to begin with, even less so once the refit timeline was cut down. We've got some lasers, countermeasures, defensive stuff."

"Unfortunately," Commissar Nix said, "that's compounded by the decision not to load up an exploratory and diplomatic ship with an overabundance of weaponry."

"Who the cack made that decision?" Campanile asked.

The captain coughed. "I believe that was the Dauphin, Midship."

The Dauphin had, until now, been occupying a quiet, dark corner of the command deck, alone with his thoughts. He stepped into the light cast by the tac table and smiled ruefully. He sighed. "I still believe this ship will find nothing but peace out there, if we could only get it out of this system."

Chapman stared at the 3D image of the *Dauntless* as it hovered over the tac table. "Zoom in here, here, and here," he said, pointing at patches along the *Dauntless'* hull. The image zoomed in to show a macro view of the hull patches he'd indicated. "Commander, can you get an analysis?"

Porvenir went to the sensor station. "Looks like a very recent repair, by the spectrograph. Slow-leaking breathables, and...thruster plasma. Sir, their upper thruster configuration looks like it was repaired on the fly. If I had a mass driver and...just a boulder-sized asteroid, I could probably knock out that whole housing. They'd be dead in the water."

"Can we hit it with our lasers?" asked the Dauphin.

Chapman shook his head. "Not without tac mirrors, sir. We currently don't have an angle."

"If only we had something big enough to throw at it," Nix offered.

"Commissar," Representative Kwan said, "let's talk to your pilot for a moment."

"Yes, sir," she replied. They climbed the ladder up to the cockpit, Chapman almost followed, but everything on this mission was at the ultimate command of the Duchess and the Dauphin, and the captain's presence wasn't explicitly requested. A brief but spirited discussion followed, though the only thing Chapman could actually make out from up there was an emphatic "ABSOLUTELY NOT" from Nix early in the conversation. They made their way back down ladder; Kwan walked stone-faced out the command deck door, and Nix returned to the tac table. It was clear that nobody was particularly happy with the plan – whatever it was – but it was going to happen anyway.

"Captain, prepare the ship for launch on the Dauphin's signal," Nix ordered.

"What signal?"

Nix glowered at the tac table. "You'll know it when you see it," she replied, avoiding eye contact with him and anyone else on the command deck.

"Acknowledged," Chapman replied. Deep breath. "Prepare to disengage remaining station-keeping modes. Navigation, prepare course Iditarod One."

32

OPERATIONS CENTER •
KESTREL BASE

"Major, boarding is unnecessary," Captain Day pleaded. "Colonel Keyes has the entire crew of the *Shoji* performing a complete sweep of the base from top to bottom. If there's anything untoward, I'm sure we'll find it."

Darinka approached the captain at the comm station. "You're afraid of her."

"Excuse me?" replied Captain Day, looking for a mute button, or the comm's audio pickup device to cover with his hand, but he was unfamiliar with the terminal.

"Your voice changes when you speak to her. Your palms begin to sweat and your ears turn red. You're afraid of her."

"That's ridiculous."

"I'd tend to agree, since over the last hour you've belittled a fleet admiral and the Duchess of a royal House, and we are far above your station. You're nervous, sure, but you're not afraid of us." She paused, arched an eyebrow. "But you are afraid of her."

"Remind me never to play poker with you."

"I prefer scopa, Captain."

"That's all very well, Captain," Major Sato replied to Day over the comm. "Nonetheless, all personnel are ordered to return to the *Shoji* immediately. That includes you, Captain."

"Acknowledged," Day replied. He turned to the Duchess. "She's getting ready to blow this place. You've all been cute with your stalling, but your time is up." He got on his comm to the *Shoji* crew. "Chuck? Get back to the ship, Major's gonna blow the base."

"Piper and I are on our way back to the ship now," Keyes replied. "I'll give the clearout order."

While Day was busy conferring with his people, Admiral Vanakar approached Darinka. "Duchess, I can't raise Lucas Wong or any of the Belt Pirates. We need to get you down to the *Pangolin*, it's your only way out of here now."

"I have to stay in the system, I have to organize the efforts here. Following the probes is Kwan's mission."

"I could put you in an escape pod but I really don't like the odds, so many things can go wrong."

Darinka looked over at the Frontier captain barking orders to his teams. "I think I have a better idea."

33

OFS DAUNTLESS · OUTSIDE KESTREL BASE

"Prepare to fire on the installation, Captain."

"Yes, Major," Captain Sakamoto replied. He licked his dry lips. "With...with what armaments, Major?"

She looked at him as if he'd just asked what the color beige tasted like. "Everything."

"Captain," called out Lieutenant Conroy, "a ship is exiting the installation's forcefield, course heading: in-system."

"Is it the *Pangolin*?" asked Sakamoto.

"Negative, Captain. It's a small ship, light leisure, Hong *Yushin*-class."

"Track it, but let it go. It's heading in-system and too small to even fit an FTL drive on. Probably someone bailing out, we can easily catch them later."

"Captain!" Major Sato whirled, bearing down on him with more fury than usual. "I'm sure the pilot of that ship has at least some information that may help our efforts."

"Ahhhh...true enough, Major. Hail the ship."

Major Sato could do nothing beyond shake her head in disbelief, and pace the bridge. She silently asked Okaasan Heika for strength to deal with this product of a slowly bloating bureaucracy.

"No response from the ship," said Lt. Conroy, "but it has come about. It's heading back toward us."

"Good, good."

"The ship is accelerating."

"What?"

"It's hitting .6c, headed straight for us. Major, it's going to ram our thrusters!"

"All defense shields to the rear quarter!" Major Sato rushed to the damage control station, knowing that it would be at the core of whatever came next.

"Brace for impact!" warned Conroy as the *Dauntless* shuddered, the lights and displays flickered, and the viewscreen lost and regained the forward view in a laterally scrolling nightmare.

Captain Sakamoto headed to the tactical station. "Can you stabilize the viewscreen?"

"It's not the viewscreen, Captain," Major Sato shot back at him. "We're in a spin, inertial dampeners are still on line. My compliments to your environmental engineering department."

"You're right," Sakamoto replied. "Tactical can't get a lock because the ship is spinning too fast."

"Not even a missile lock?" Sato asked.

"What do you think?" Sakamoto asked the tactical officer.

"I definitely won't be able to get a clean lock," she replied. "But I'll do my best."

Conroy pointed at the side-scrolling viewscreen. "Major, the *Pangolin*!"

"Ensign," shouted the Major, "do your best."

The ensign at the tactical station aimed the targeting joystick on the escaping *Pangolin*, painted the target, and pulled the trigger.

34

OFS SHOJI • OUTSIDE KESTREL BASE

Captain Day was yet again on the comm, this time trying to prevent a suicide. "Admiral, I'm not gonna tell you again. Get on this ship, now. You have my word, neither you or the Duchess will be a prisoner."

"Negative, Captain."

The crew prepared the ship for emergency launch. "Your rogue ship's halfway to Outpost Orange already. You've won, I hope you're happy. Now they're gonna blow this rock to bits. Get in, I can't stall any longer."

Keyes nudged his way past the captain, securing the bridge crew in their acceleration straps. "Graf, we have to go now."

"Captain." This was their esteemed passenger, the Duchess Ravenscar, secured in the seat next to the captain. She shook her head. "She's not going to leave. We should go."

"Five seconds to launch. Cack!" he exclaimed, kicking an access panel while securing himself into his station.

"Ten demerits, Captain," the Taisei said.

Piper called out from the rear of the bridge, "Cap, *Dauntless* is firing missiles."

Day checked his tactical display. "It's spinning like a top, there's no way it can get a lock."

"Emergency launch initiated," the Taisei declared.

The *Shoji* shot out of Cartesia's ring system at a burst of .8c. In a moment, they were long gone from Cartesia. Now cruising in open space, they were back in contact with the Imperial comm network.

"What are our orders, Taisei?" Day asked in a strained voice, as the aftereffect of more Gs than the ship's inertial dampeners could handle washed over the crew.

"Processing...You are to return your passenger to Cerigo, after which you will return to Gorobei to be debriefed."

Debriefed at the Bastion. He didn't like the sound of that.

As the crew unbuckled from their harnesses, the captain was approached by the Duchess.

"All right people, you heard the Taisei. Best speed to Cerigo. Duchess, we'll have you home by morning."

"Captain, you mustn't feel responsible for Admiral Vanakar. She was the last Federation dignitary left, her presence at Kestrel Base legally guaranteed the Federation's existence and presence on the base. It was her duty to stay behind for as long as possible. I'll send a team back for her as soon as I get home."

"You guys, you just don't get it, do you? You're sending people out into open space, and you don't even know what's out there. No, not even - you know what's out there. We already fought a whole war against what's out there, and you're going to remind them we're still here."

"There's no evidence the Sanzoku are still a threat."

"No evidence they're not, either."

"Captain, humanity is dying, whether they know it yet or not. We need-"

"You need to fix your own civilization before you spread it around the galaxy like a plague."

"What about your civilization?"

"We know enough to quarantine ourselves, for our benefit and the galaxy's."

"Well, Captain," she said diplomatically, "I don't share your narrow view, but at least now I understand it."

Captain Day turned away from the Duchess to look at his station's readouts. "Six hours thirteen minutes to Cerigo, Duchess. It's been a long day; I recommend you get some sleep. As I have a shift here on the bridge, my quarters are available."

"Thank you, Captain."

The Duchess left the bridge, leaving Captain Day with nothing but his thoughts.

He shook his head, muttering to himself, "They have no idea what they've gotten us into."

35

THE PROSCENIUM · OFS DAUNTLESS · KESTREL BASE

The epilogue to Major Sato's illustrious career had ended in disgrace. The mission was a failure. That much was for certain.

The *Pangolin* was on its way out of the system. Kestrel Base was burning in space. All they had to show for their efforts was a brig full of Belt pirates and the likely wreck of the *Dauntless*.

Their first priority had been to restore the Proscenium, their primary comm system. Once accomplished (audio only was the best that could be done under the circumstances), they entered the Proscenium and requested their orders. The Pontifex himself replied, and he had no patience for the usual pleasantries.

"Captain Francis Decker Sakamoto, you are hereby relieved of command of Outbound Fleet Ship *Dauntless*, designation YKY-885. Please return to Gorobei for debriefing as soon as possible." Captain Sakamoto stood at attention, sobbing in disgrace.

It was disgusting.

"Command of OFS *Dauntless* is to be transferred to Captain Enos Edward Conroy, promoted from First Lieutenant. Captain Conroy is to return the *Dauntless* to Satsuma Shipyard for disposition."

Major Sato liked Conroy; his promotion was a good decision on the part of Fleet Command, in her opinion.

"Major Vivian Sato, you are to return to Gorobei for debrief and reassignment. First, please accompany Captain Sakamoto to ensure his timely debriefing."

She sighed, and hoped the shuttle ride home was a fast one.

36

OFS SHOJI · VIP LANDING PAD 2 · HAUPSTADT · CERIGO

"Under the current political climate, there's simply no way," Speaker Okwende said.

Kwan Li had been dead for half a day, and already their plans were falling apart without him.

This part of the plan should have been simple. Darinka would ask the League for a small fleet of ships, advertise for volunteers to be pioneers of a new frontier, and they'd head out there. A fresh start for the human race, far away from the nonsense of the solar system.

Instead, their actions had only made things worse.

Executive Chen, not generally known to be an emotional man, had quite simply lost his mind. He blamed Okwende and the Duchess for the Dauphin's untimely demise; his reaction was to remove the Hong Dominion Corporation from the League of Worlds and he was reportedly awfully close to declaring war on Der Zweiwelten. He did, however, immediately declare war on the Frontier Territories, despite the strenuous protestations of innocence administered by Envoy Stringfellow.

Somewhere in the midst of all those proceedings, the now 17 (or so) provisional states of the Primary found time for a brief, perfunctory parliamentary measure to consider the Satellite Federation to be dissolved. It was the only thing they all seemed to be able to agree on.

"What can we do in the meantime, Speaker?" Darinka asked. "There's a lot riding on the success of this mission. And I need to make sure Kwan's sacrifice wasn't for naught."

"I understand, and," he paused, "I sympathize, but I've got too much on my plate at the moment, Duchess. If I'm unable to keep the peace long-term, the League may fail. Maintaining the League has to be my first priority. If I see a way to help you, I'll absolutely take it. But everyone is too busy preparing for war right now to even consider your version of peace." With that very negative thought, Okwende reluctantly signed off. Her thoughts immediately went to Kwan; she pushed them away. This was no time to go soft.

"Did you even have a Plan B?" Captain Day asked.

"Captain! I'm sorry, I didn't know you were...in the habit of listening in on personal conversations."

"I would have knocked, but you're in my quarters, ma'am. I came to let you know that we're home." He quickly added, "Your home, anyway."

Perhaps this lost Frontier rube could be of some use. A fresh perspective could yield some unexpected insights. "What do you think we should do, Captain?"

"I dunno. Get some breakfast, for sure. Maybe you can show me around the palace before I leave?" He flashed a winning smile.

She chose to deflect this latest flippant response, though she was surprised to find that it pleased her to have a conversation with someone who for once didn't seem to care about the trappings of protocol. "You do make a good point; I am hungry. But I meant what we should do in a larger sense. Regarding the situation we just barely lived through."

He shook his head. "That ship is already lost. They won't make it ten light years before they end up a smear of ether grease on some alien ship's hull. There's no guarantees, but if the Sanzoku War taught us anything, it's that you shouldn't leave the solar system without the largest battlefleet you can find."

"Peace through superior firepower?"

"Something like that."

"How well did that work at the Prahari Line?"

He shook his head. "We still don't know what that was."

"Well, we know what it wasn't: a victory, for either side." Still, bellicose as he was, he did give her an idea. A few, even. "Captain, would you like to stay here for a while?"

37

SFS PANGOLIN • RED ROUTE
ONE • 18 HOURS OUTSIDE THE
SOLAR SYSTEM

Captain Chapman sat at the Navigation station on the command deck, idly watching the ship's progress as the *Pangolin* progressed along Red Route One, the trail laid out by the first of the Iditarod Probes.

The command deck was empty, except for him, as he'd dismissed the crew for the first two shifts. The XLRs and the probe data from *Anchorage-1* showed absolutely nothing for the next few days, so he'd ordered the crew to get some quality rack time. Commissar Nix had initially hung around for a few hours, but eventually even she realized that her time was best spent elsewhere.

Cassini had settled into her new home in the cockpit. Engineering crews had installed a small bubbler unit inside, and tweaked the layout to allow her direct access to the quarter deck reclamator one level below.

Chapman had climbed up to check on the pilot. She was initially unresponsive, lost in a reverie inspired by the light show outside the cockpit's canopy caused by the FTL drive. The ship flew so fast that the space grease it cut through was burned away, the reaction creating an amorphous puddle of shimmering rainbows washing over the canopy.

"Do you see it, Cap?"

"I see it. How's it going up here?"

"The ship's good, currently making 1.38c en route to probe contact designated ANC-1. Estimated time: eight days. Propulsion and navigation systems are green straight down the line."

"Very well," he replied. "How are you doing?"

"I'm alright. I think FTL travel is making me a little more philosophical than I used to be. I just find myself staring into the colors, getting all kinds of lost, to be honest."

"Let's not get too lost, ok, Pilot?"

"Understood. I should have my bearings within a day or two."

"If you feel the need to see Dr. Abdelaziz, don't hesitate. That's why he's here."

"Will do, Cap."

"Al right, as you were. Enjoy the show."

He climbed back down to the command deck to find Porvenir checking the Operations station readouts.

"Hey, Cap," she greeted him without turning around, "we've got auxiliary environmental systems running off backup power instead of secondary. Crews working too fast in gravdock." She worked the controls, rerouting the power. "I saw Campanile on my way here, she's coming down to relieve you in a few minutes, but I can stick around if you want to rack out now."

The prospect of sleep after being awake for the equivalent of four straight shifts - eventful shifts - sounded awfully good to the captain at that moment. "Commander, I think I'll take you up on that."

"*Pangolin*," Porvenir addressed the ship, "transfer command to Lieutenant Commander Porvenir, as of 05:18 ship time."

"Does current commanding officer confirm?"

"Confirmed, authorization Ibex five-seven Acorn." Chapman thought for a moment. "Any way we can disable that? Or streamline the process?"

She considered the request. "Maybe. It's a security thing, though; I'll have to talk to the Commissar about it."

"Whatever. I'm going to sleep for a few days. Try not to let the place fall apart while I'm gone."

"That's the idea, Cap."

Chapman left the command deck and shuffled toward his quarters. Halfway there, he saw Campanile's drake walking toward him from the corridor's ceiling, its talons making small indentations as it made its way along the makeit conduit. His initial thought was to catch the thing and send it out an airlock, but he was just too tired.

His quarters were once again a bit of a mess, but that could wait. Captain Houlihan's bomber jacket had somehow made its way to the floor, though, and that wouldn't do; he placed it on one of the hooks near the door, admiring the new Project Iditarod patch on the sleeve.

Losing the Dauphin wasn't a huge blow to their immediate mission; between Chapman and Commissar Nix, they had a firm grasp on how to proceed. But the plan was his, the motivation was his, the will to make this happen was originally his. He deserved to see his dream come to fruition, but instead he'd had to sacrifice himself to give that dream a fighting chance.

Chapman tried not to think about Kwan Li, just as he tried not to think about the look of impotent horror in the eyes of the Chamberlain in his final moments, before Okaasan Heika - or whatever it was - melted him into slag. He tried not to think about the Prahari Line, and why he was the only one from that entire coalition fleet left alive.

Maybe, somewhere out in the black, he might find the answer.

As Chapman sat and removed his boots he found his boot flask, forgotten in all the excitement of the previous day. He stashed the flask in a desk drawer that was filled with a bunch of junk he never used. Before closing the drawer, though, he saw an item from his past: a clockwork bird that Lex had bought for him while they were on Cerigo. He placed it on his desk.

He reclined into bed, still wearing his uniform. Force of habit from his XO days. "Lights out," he said, and the *Pangolin*'s computer complied, leaving no light but the cabin's various control panels emitting a subdued, cool blue glow.

Captain Chapman stared up into the darkness, exhausted, and was asleep in seconds. He allowed himself to finally dream again, for the first time in years; dreams of new worlds, and the flags that would claim them.

38

HANGAR THREE • THE BASTION • GOROBEI

The ornate entrance to the Bastion was carved by industrial lasers into the side of a massive rock outcrop, inspired vaguely by ancient temple designs at pre-Egress Yaodong sites like Petra, Athens and Futenma. Major Sato herself piloted the shuttle through the entrance and landed the craft; the dishonored Captain Sakamoto was a useless, blubbering mess on the floor in the shuttle's hold. She'd taken the extra precaution of restraining him at the wrists to avoid any attempt at seppuku; the disgraced had been known to practice it on very rare occasions, and while Sato felt sure that thoughts of Sakamoto's family's welfare would prevent him from doing anything untoward, she also hadn't gotten where she was today by being sloppy.

They stepped out of the shuttle into a small craft hangar, the walls appointed in mosaics of Mitsuko Katayama's adventures during the late Colonial Wars, leading the old Frontier Territories to become the strong, mighty Kintsugi Nation that now held sway over a hundred million souls. A band of The Next, personal servants of Okaasan Heika whose heads were completely encased in opaque helmets, met the officers a few steps from the shuttle. The Next parted to allow the Pontifex to approach.

"Your service honors us," the Pontifex told the officers as they disembarked. "Mr. Sakamoto, please follow The Next. They will lead you to what follows." Wordlessly, his head hung low with shame, the shell of the man once known as Captain Sakamoto shuffled off with tiny footsteps, as if he'd regressed fully to childhood during the shuttle trip.

The man was an absolute embarrassment, Sato thought.

"Major, please come with me to the Orrery. Okaasan Heika would like to put this Iditarod situation behind us as soon as possible."

The Major silently followed the Pontifex; the cavernous ceilings of the corridors made her feel insignificant, as was their intent. As they entered the Orrery, they walked into the midst of a holographic display of Albion and its moon system. "Pontifex, before we go on I must begin with the strongest of apologies-"

"Unnecessary, Major," replied a disembodied voice. Albion and its satellites coalesced into the form of a woman. She was of slight build, robed and hooded, holding in each of her upraised hands the Kintsugi Nation's main planets, Tennosei and Kennosei, their moons orbiting them like small insects. Major Sato immediately fell to one knee and bowed her head, as did the Pontifex. "The failure of the *Dauntless* is not yours," the holographic woman said. "However as ranking officer charged with this mission's oversight, I do concede that it is your responsibility. Rest assured; you will be given an opportunity to rectify the situation."

"Heika, this moment is my life's greatest honor."

"It is, Major." Okaasan Heika tucked her holographic hands into her holographic sleeves, and her worlds left to find their places in the solar system now circulating above her. "However, in the interest of your mission, I suggest we return to the honorifics later and deal with the matter at hand, dear one."

"Of course, Heika. The...*Pangolin* is still following Red Route One?"

"It is indeed, Major."

"Your Grace, I beg of you; give me the fastest ship we have, and I'll have the *Pangolin*'s hull outside the Bastion by dinner."

"I believe Okaasan Heika had in mind something without her fingerprints all over it," the Pontifex interjected.

"The Pontifex is correct," Okaasan Heika told the Major. "I have already accrued far too much exposure in this matter. The *Pangolin* is outside of the solar system, but still in range of the Kuiper Defense Grid."

"It's ironic, really," mused the Pontifex. "After the Sanzoku War, we developed the grid to protect the system from outside attack. I never dreamed we might use the grid offensively."

"Your dreamlessness is one of your many failings, Pontifex." Okaasan Heika's image was replaced by that of the Kuiper Marches, the ring of rocks and ice at the outermost edge of the solar system. Green dots within the marches represented the Defense Grid. A straight red line going out of the solar system, into infinity, represented Red Route One. The blue dot traveling that line was the *Pangolin*.

A yellow line began moving out from one of the green dots, eventually connecting with the blue dot. "By my calculations," said the now-disembodied Okaasan Heika, "our FTL mass driver launch should have been effective."

"Should have been, Heika?"

"Find their wreckage. Verify their destruction. Complete it, if necessary. If this affair is stopped early enough, all parties involved can still deny it ever happened."

"Immediately, Heika." Major Sato very nearly ran back to the hangar.

"Pontifex," said Okaasan Heika, "ensure that the very enthusiastic major has a fast ship and a good crew for this assignment."

"Your Grace, do you think the *Pangolin*...was detected?"

Okaasan Heika seemed to consider the question for a long moment. "I think we've not seen the last of the Sanzoku, Pontifex. Not by a long shot."

So many Dans to thank…

First and foremost, extensive thanks go to Dan Keel. His bartending skills are rivaled only by his ability to wrangle this text into something coherent. I am honored to call him a friend, and beyond grateful for his contributions in editing this book.

I would not be whatever it is I am today without the many decades of friendship and adventure I've shared with the legendary Dan Carter. The stories are true. The legend is real. The future is unwritten. Apologies, once again, to Marky Ramone; we didn't mean to scare you.

And especially, thanks to my lovely wife Danielle. Her love and patience are seemingly endless, and without those qualities this book would not exist. Heck, I probably would not exist.

Thanks also to the beta readers: Knowlton Dee, Keith Zunda, Joey DeCrescenzo and Rachel Russell (who also helped with some Japanese terminology); photographer extraordinaire Jon DeNicholas; military advisor Brig. Gen. John A. Butch (Ret.) of the Courdevans Defence Force; Mike Watson at Aberdyne, for agreeing to take a chance on *The Pangolin Republic*; my parents and grandparents; and my brother Tony, sister Diana and her husband Chris, who were always up for whatever nonsense I was getting into creatively.

If your name isn't here, don't worry – this is only book one.

Michael Moutinho (mo-TEEN-yo) enjoys long walks on the beach, puppies, and single malt scotch. He lives in southern New England with his wife and an indeterminate number of dogs. This is his first published novel.